Jack Cameron

Copyright © 2015 Jack Cameron
All rights reserved.

ISBN: 1515094022
ISBN 13: 978-1515094029

The Fight

Chapter 1

Nick Sullivan staggered to his feet in the gathering darkness as the initial Fourth of July fireworks began to light up the sky behind him. Sand from the lakeside beach matted on his face and hair. Blood was seeping from a cut over his right eye, and his head ached. He spit some sand out of his mouth and slipped his tongue over a loose tooth. Both of his hands were covered with blood, too—he wasn't sure if the blood belonged to him or the guy at his feet. He'd been in a few fights in his eighteen years, but this had been the toughest.

The man on his hands and knees gasping for air weighed close to 250 pounds and sported a shaved head and a long beard. Known to friends and foes alike as Tiny, he was wearing a black-leather vest with "Satan's Knights" stitched in red on the back. Nick and Tiny were embroiled in a fierce battle that was half fistfight, half wrestling match. It had been going on for about forty-five seconds, but it felt to Nick like the fight had lasted fifteen minutes. Nick believed the brawl was just about over when he shoved a bull-rushing Tiny to the ground and then delivered three hard kicks to his stomach. With Tiny temporarily out of action with the wind knocked out of him, Nick turned his attention to the fight taking place about thirty feet to his left.

His friend, Owen Anderson, was also going at it with a guy wearing a Satan's Knights vest, but Owen wasn't faring as well as Nick had. While Nick was a sturdy six foot two, 220 pounds, and in great shape, Owen was fifty pounds lighter. Just as important to the outcome of this fight, Owen didn't have the same fiery temper Nick did—a temper that sometimes got Nick into trouble but just as often helped get him out of it. The guy Owen was fighting went by the name Vukie. He had long, black hair tied in a ponytail, topped by a red do-rag, and both of his arms and his neck were completely covered with tattoos. Though not as big as Tiny, Vukie still outweighed Owen by about forty pounds. Owen was getting his ass kicked.

Nick watched as Vukie punched Owen in the stomach and then, with Owen doubled over from that punch, delivered a vicious kick to Owen's left side. Owen gasped in pain and fell to the sand, one of his ribs fractured.

Nick, worried about Owen and about to run to his aid, glanced back to make sure Tiny was still incapacitated. While Nick was momentarily distracted by the Vukie-Owen fight, Tiny had gotten to his feet and taken a chain from his back pocket. The chain was only about eighteen inches long, but the links were thick and heavy, and it weighed at least twenty pounds. Tiny was just winding up to swing the chain when Nick turned back toward him.

As the chain swung in a lateral arc toward Nick's head, Nick ducked and charged Tiny with his shoulder lowered. A split second after the chain glanced off Nick's upper back, Nick drove into Tiny at full speed, knocking them both to the ground. Nick was so enraged, so fueled with adrenaline, that he would later have only a vague memory of what followed. Tiny and Nick rolled around briefly in the sand, trading blows, Nick using his fists and Tiny swinging his chain. After absorbing two more hits with the chain, Nick managed to grab the other end of it. Clinging to opposite ends of the chain, trying to wrest it from each other, both men struggled to their feet.

As Nick and Tiny continued to tug on the chain, Nick suddenly kicked Tiny hard in the groin. Tiny doubled over in pain; Nick jerked the chain free and, in one motion, swung it back around at Tiny. Nick had been aiming in the general direction of his midsection, but as Tiny pitched forward, stunned by the kick to his groin, the hurtling chain ripped into his neck. The force of Nick's blow, combined with the rough edges of some of the links in the chain, ripped a jagged chunk of flesh out of Tiny's throat. A geyser of blood erupted from his neck as he fell to the ground, screaming.

Owen had gamely continued his fight with Vukie while Nick and Tiny had been battling over the chain, repeatedly getting up after Vukie knocked him down. Vukie had just slammed him to the ground again when Owen heard Tiny's scream. Both Vukie and Owen turned to see Tiny lying on the beach, blood spurting from his neck. It took only about fifteen seconds for his body to go completely still.

Vukie looked at the chain in Nick's hand and wanted no part of that. Any doubts he had about what to do next vanished as he heard voices approaching from the walkway leading to the beach. He ran toward the other end of the small beach and disappeared into the surrounding woods.

Owen rose to one knee, wracked in pain and only semicoherent. The low-hanging moon reflected over the shimmering lake and bathed Tiny's lifeless body in an eerie light. As Owen lapsed into unconsciousness, he wondered whether it had really been only ten minutes earlier that he and Nick had been surrounded by friends at a party, enjoying themselves, without a care in the world.

Growing Up

Chapter 2

Nick Sullivan, Owen Anderson, Dante Lombardo, and Ryan Cunningham had been friends since childhood. The movies sometimes depict a group of three or four kids as best friends from elementary school all the way through high school, but it seldom happens that way in real life. Kids evolve as they grow up, develop different interests at different times, mature at dissimilar rates. Sometimes your best friends for a period of time are based more on who's on your baseball team or who sits near you in class in a particular year than on anything more profound than that.

Nick, Owen, Dante, and Ryan all had Mrs. Brogan for kindergarten and became friends then. It wouldn't be accurate to say the group had been intact throughout their school years. But even as one or two of them had drifted from the inner circle into other cliques for a couple of years, they all remained friendly with each other. And at least two of them—though which two it was varied over time—always stuck together, exerting a gravitational pull on the wayward members of the group that eventually succeeded in drawing all four of them together again.

The boys grew up in Pennington, New Hampshire, a moderately affluent town of about twenty thousand people located ten miles south of Manchester, the state's largest city. Though Pennington was considered a suburb of Manchester, its residents working in the tech companies sprinkled along Route 495 just across the border in Massachusetts outnumbered the folks who actually worked in Manchester. Like many of the towns in southern New Hampshire, Pennington had grown significantly in the previous decade, with much of the growth fueled by former Massachusetts residents attracted to the proximity to lakes and mountains and the absence of a state income tax.

    For outdoorsy or active kids, Pennington and its surrounding area had much to offer. Skiing was very popular in New Hampshire. Pennington residents placing a premium on convenience could find numerous ski resorts within a forty-five-minute drive. The more serious skiers could venture farther north into the White Mountains, which featured not only the highest peak and fiercest winds in the Northeast but also some of its best and most challenging skiing.

    If the White Mountains were the spine of New Hampshire, Lake Winnipesaukee could be regarded as the state's heart, both geographically and culturally. The southern shores of Lake Winnipesaukee were a little over an hour's drive from Pennington. Spanning roughly seventy square miles, the lake was dotted with more than 250 islands. Although the lake was popular for snowmobiling, skating, and ice fishing in the winter, it truly became a mecca for visitors in the summer. The houses lining the lake, both second homes and rental properties, ranged from simple cottages to opulent estates. With hundreds of miles of shoreline and a seemingly endless expanse of water for boating, swimming, and other aquatic activities, Lake Winnipesaukee was considered by most Pennington residents—as well as many others all over New England—to be a preferable alternative to the frigid waters of the Maine coast or the traffic-choked journey to Cape Cod.

The town of Pennington itself also had much to offer kids growing up there. There were youth leagues in town for all the popular sports, almost all of which were run by well-intentioned and qualified—if sometimes overzealous—parents. There was no scarcity of fields or gyms for the kids to use. The town also featured an indoor pool, two outdoor pools, and a gymnastics academy. There was no question, however, that the crown jewel of Pennington's athletic facilities was the Ice Palace. Opened the year the four boys were born, after two years of political wrangling and fund-raising, the Ice Palace was a glistening hockey complex that housed two rinks and an off-ice training facility. Three of the four friends would spend a large chunk of their formative years within the frigid confines of that building.

* * *

It was evident from the time he was very young that Nick Sullivan was a hockey prodigy. Like most Pennington kids who wanted to learn to play hockey—or, more accurately, whose parents wanted them to learn to play hockey—Nick, Owen, and Ryan participated in the learn-to-skate program at the Ice Palace when they were four years old, and then graduated to a hockey instructional program the following year, the same year they entered kindergarten. The instructional sessions took place each Saturday and Sunday morning, from November through March, and consisted primarily of training in hockey fundamentals and a series of drills intended to hone both skating skills and stick skills. No competitive games were played, although intrasquad scrimmages were sometimes held in the last fifteen minutes of the sessions. These scrimmages were intentionally informal and low-key—the parent-instructors served as goalies, there were sometimes as many as eight or nine players per team on the ice at once, and no one kept score (except some of the particularly intense parents seated in the stands).

    Even as a five-year-old playing in those ragtag scrimmages, Nick stood out. His hockey prowess would come as no surprise to those who knew his parents' athletic backgrounds. Nick was the oldest of Matt and Chris Sullivan's three children, and the only boy. Matt had been a three-sport athlete in high school, captaining both the football team—playing tight end and linebacker—and the hockey team—as a hard-hitting defenseman—during his senior year. He went on to play football at Merrimack College, a Division II school in North Andover, Massachusetts, although a series of knee injuries would limit his success on the field there.

Nick's real athletic pedigree was on his mother's side of the family. His uncle Cam, his mom's older brother, had played ten years of minor-league baseball, making brief appearances in the big leagues as an outfielder with both the Cubs and the Orioles. Chris's greatest athletic success had come as a field-hockey player—she was the all-time leading scorer at the University of New Hampshire and had been one of the last three players cut from the national team that was heading for the 1980 Olympic games in Moscow before a US-led international boycott kept all the American teams at home that summer. Her sporting abilities extended beyond field hockey, though; Chris was one of those people who was good at any athletic endeavor she attempted. At UNH she also played varsity basketball, excelled at intramural tennis, and was a legendary beer-pong player. Even as an adult, her talents remained undiminished. She took up golf in her thirties and was soon besting her husband at it, and woe to the man who challenged her to a game of pool at a friend's house or local pub.

To the mostly untrained eyes of the parents shivering in the Ice Palace stands during the instructional program's drills and scrimmages, it was clear that Nick was the best player on the ice, though it wasn't exactly clear why that was the case. When a group of kids went into the corner or along the boards to retrieve a puck, Nick was almost always the kid who skated out with it. When the kids did a keep-away drill, it was Nick who invariably kept control of the puck the longest. If the puck was passed toward the front of the net—sometimes intentionally, sometimes haphazardly—during a scrimmage, it was usually Nick who was in the best position to corral it and shoot it on goal. How he managed to do all that was less obvious. Nick didn't appear to be that much faster, bigger, or stronger than the other players. It was his more subtle talents—his hand-eye coordination, his knack for being in the right place at the right time, and his relentlessness—that set him apart.

Almost all kids in Pennington stayed in the instructional program for two years and moved up to the travel teams, which played real games against other southern New Hampshire towns, when they reached age seven. The youth leagues in New Hampshire were organized by age level; seven- and eight-year-olds played on Mite teams, and nine- and ten-year-olds played on Squirt teams, with older kids eventually moving up through the Pee-wee, Bantam, and Midget levels. Most participating towns, other than the very small ones, skated more than one team in each age bracket—a few of the larger towns had six or seven teams at each of the younger levels—and allocated their players among those teams based on their performances in preseason tryouts. Pennington, for example, typically had three Mite teams: the Mite As, Mite Bs and Mite Cs. The top fourteen to sixteen performers in the tryouts were placed on the Mite As, and they played the top Mite teams from other towns; the next fourteen to sixteen players made up the Mite Bs, who played other towns' mid-tier Mite teams; and so on.

When Nick's first year in the instructional program ended in March, the guy who ran the program told Nick's parents he was ready to try out for one of Pennington's Mite teams for the following season. That suggestion introduced a bit of controversy into the Sullivan household. Although Matt and Chris didn't actively disagree on the matter, they weren't exactly on the same page. Matt was leaning toward the notion of keeping Nick in the instructional program for another year; he saw the value of Nick's staying with his friends and wondered whether Nick was really ready to compete with kids two years older. Chris, who was more driven than her husband by nature, had no such reservations. She recognized that Nick had talent, maybe special talent, and was in favor of whatever would best develop that.

Matt and Chris debated—without ever actually arguing over—the matter on and off for about a week before they even told Nick about the opportunity to try out for the Mites. Eventually they agreed they wouldn't force Nick to move up to the Mites, and he would attend the Mites tryouts only if he wanted to. Matt found himself mildly surprised that Chris acquiesced to that arrangement. Chris, however, knew intuitively that the combination of Nick's competitive spirit and the trust that a six-year-old reposes in his parents meant it wouldn't be too difficult to convince Nick to try out for the Mites.

Initially Nick was a bit reluctant to move up to the Mites. A friendly kid with an easy smile, Nick was very popular among his peers. He enjoyed playing in the instructional program with his friends and classmates, and that feeling was reciprocated, particularly from Owen and Ryan. Over the course of a few weeks, though, Chris—without ever coming out and saying to Nick that she was in favor of it—subtly extolled the virtues of playing on the Mites. She emphasized that he'd make new friends while still keeping all of his old friends.

"You'd still get to spend a lot of time with Owen and Ryan," she told him. "After all, you see Dante a lot, and he doesn't even play hockey."

She talked about how exciting it would be to travel around the state, playing different towns. And she reminded him that he sometimes got bored going through the instructional drills that he had mastered weeks earlier. By the time sign-ups for Mite tryouts rolled around in May, Nick was genuinely excited about moving up to the Mites.

The tryouts were scheduled for a Tuesday and a Thursday evening in early August. They were being run by the president of the Pennington Youth Hockey League, who had enlisted three other youth-team coaches to assist him in evaluating the players. About fifty kids showed up for the Tuesday session, almost all of whom had at least one parent watching from the stands. Matt and Chris both attended. They had expected Nick to be a little nervous (they both were), but Nick just seemed genuinely excited to be back playing hockey. Although a few parents commented on the absurdity of bundling up for the cold of a hockey rink on a ninety-degree day, few seemed to mind being there. Many of the kids trying out had played on one of the Mite teams the previous year, and those parents tended to band together, discussing in low tones which kids had the best chances of making the A team.

Later that night Matt and Chris talked over Nick's performance and his chances of making the A or B team. Nick had skated well, they both agreed, and did not look out of place competing against kids a year or two older. Chris was, however, a bit surprised when she took a call from the league president the next day—before the Thursday session—informing her that Nick had made the A team and didn't even need to come to the second tryout.

Chapter 3

In many small New England towns, there's one family that seems to be both known and held in high regard throughout the town. The parents are an important part of the professional and social fabric of the town, and the children become known for their athletic and/or academic achievements. In Pennington, that family was the Andersons.

Mark Anderson, Owen's father, was born and raised in Pennington. His father had been a cop in Manchester and was revered by Mark and his two brothers. For a long time, Mark planned to follow in his father's footsteps, and he majored in criminal justice at Northeastern University in Boston. Continually encouraged by his parents to strive for something better than their own lot in life, Mark ended up attending Boston College Law School. After graduating from there with honors, he had offers to join a number of prestigious law firms in Boston. The tug of his hometown roots was strong, however, and for Mark it was a relatively easy decision to return to Pennington and start a career there.

One of the ties Mark felt to Pennington was his girlfriend, Bridget Callahan, who had also been raised there. Mark and Bridget were about to be married, so it wasn't that Mark needed to return to Pennington in order to be close to her. But he found alluring the notion of settling in a town where they had both grown up, where they both knew so many people, and where they both had so many memories.

Mark and Bridget had been classmates at St. Xavier High School in Pennington and began dating their senior year there. With Mark heading to Northeastern and Bridget attending college in western Massachusetts, they decided to break up before going away to school. Despite the breakup, they maintained a relationship throughout their college years that neither of them could fully understand, much less explain. They did not regard themselves as boyfriend and girlfriend, and they both dated other people during college. They talked by phone occasionally while away at school, however, and saw each other frequently when back in Pennington over the summer or during Christmas break. Sometimes their get-togethers in Pennington consisted of lunches or dinners as friends, while other times they let their feelings and hormones turn them into more than that. Both Mark and Bridget were tired of their parents and friends asking them what was going on between them, because neither of them really knew. They did realize, though, that there was some bond between them that had not been severed by time, distance, or romantic interludes with others.

After graduation, with Mark entering law school at Boston College, Bridget took a job teaching at a private high school in Boston. Bridget always denied—even to Mark—that her decision to accept that particular job was influenced in any way by its proximity to Mark, but in reality they were both delighted to be living in the same city. They began dating "officially" soon after Bridget moved to Boston and became engaged just before Mark finished law school.

Mark interviewed with the largest law firm in Manchester, whose appeal to him lay not only in its sterling reputation but also in the fact that it had branch offices in several of the towns surrounding Manchester, including Pennington. When the firm extended Mark an offer, his first inquiry was whether he could be assigned to the Pennington office. Assured that he could be, Mark enthusiastically accepted the offer. Mark built a practice there that centered on estate planning, trusts, and personal taxes, with the bulk of his clientele comprised of fellow Pennington residents. He developed a reputation in the community as a trusted source of not just good legal work but also practical advice and sound judgment.

* * *

Owen was the first of Mark and Bridget's four children, born three years into their marriage. Bridget, who had been teaching third grade in Pennington, left her position after Owen was born, as she wanted to be home with the baby and also because she and Mark were planning on additional children. Twin daughters and another son followed within the next few years.

Owen was, in many ways, the stereotypical first child. As his parents, of necessity, devoted more time to his infant siblings than to him, he learned self-reliance at an early age. He was also a rule follower. Those traits, combined with his natural intelligence and easygoing demeanor, led teachers and neighbors to think of him as the ideal child. It was an assessment that Mark and Bridget found little reason to dispute.

As he approached his teen years, Owen was already exhibiting many of the traits that would define him as an adult. He was a straight-A student, a harbinger of the later academic success that would pave the way for him to embark on a successful business career. He was also well liked by his peers, which, given the somewhat skewed social priorities of middle schoolers, is not always typical of the smartest kid in the class.

Perhaps most striking were Owen's leadership traits. Whenever a group project was assigned in school, almost all of the kids in the class wanted to work with Owen on it—not so much because he was smart (there were other bright kids in the class who were much less sought out) but because everyone knew that Owen would organize and lead the project in a way others could not.

Owen never seemed to shy away from exerting his leadership skills, even when that involved dealing with difficult situations. During seventh grade, Pennington Middle School committed to fielding a lacrosse team for the first time if enough boys signed up. Owen led the charge in recruiting kids to play. More significantly, after a season in which a twenty-three-year-old first-time coach sucked all the fun out of the sport by constantly and profanely berating his players during practices, it was

Owen who organized a small group that met with the middle-school principal to request a different coach for the following season. Everyone wants to be CEO on payday, but not many want to be CEO when it comes time to make the hard choice between falling short of budget or laying off 15 percent of the workforce to save expenses. Owen embraced the role of leader in both good and bad times.

* * *

By the time Owen was in middle school, the Anderson family had established quite a footprint in town. Mark's law practice was thriving, he was coaching youth football, and he was president of Pennington Little League (a thankless position that could be survived only by a man of Mark's patience and good humor). Bridget, who had established a reputation as one of the better teachers in town, considered returning to teaching after her youngest child entered kindergarten. She ultimately decided against that, as she wanted to be home for her kids. She did, however, successfully run for school committee and found time to help with fund-raising for some new playing fields to be built in town.

The veneer of success and wholesomeness surrounding the Andersons, however, masked some fissures in the foundation. One member of Pennington's first family was wrestling with some personal turmoil.

Chapter 4

Ryan loved the New England Patriots. Long a National Football League doormat, the Patriots were just beginning their rise to respectability under Coach Bill Parcells as Ryan was getting old enough to develop a rooting interest in football. His devotion to the team became set in stone when, as a ten-year-old, he watched their unexpected run to the Super Bowl following the 1996 season.

One Sunday afternoon, two seasons after the Patriots' Super Bowl trip, Ryan was sitting in the living room of his father's apartment, watching the Patriots play the New York Jets. Like all ardent Patriots fans, Ryan hated the Jets. The Patriots were trailing 28–27 midway through the fourth quarter when Ryan's father, Darren, came home and joined Ryan in the living room to check out the score.

With just over a minute to play in the game, Drew Bledsoe connected with Troy Brown on what looked like a game-winning twenty-four-yard touchdown pass. Ryan whooped with joy. He was surprised to see his father kick over the hassock in front of him and blurt out "Goddamn it!"

"Dad, I thought you were a Pats fan," Ryan said questioningly.

"I am. Don't worry about it," his father muttered.

Ryan's puzzlement quickly turned to dismay when he heard the TV announcer report that there was a penalty flag on the play—holding on the Patriots—and the touchdown was being called back. He checked out his father's reaction out of the corner of his eye and saw him smile broadly.

After two more plays that yielded only six yards, the Patriots lined up for a forty-five-yard field goal attempt with only five seconds left in the game. Ryan held his breath as the kick sailed toward the uprights. When he saw that the kick was good, winning the game for the Patriots, he refrained from any overt celebration, afraid of pissing off his father. His father, though, stunned him once again by shouting "Yeah!" and clapping his hands twice.

"So you weren't really for the Jets?" Ryan asked.

"No, you know I hate the fuckin' Jets."

"But how come you were mad when the Patriots scored that TD?"

"I wanted the Pats to win," Darren said, as if this should be obvious to everyone. "I just needed them to win by less than four points."

Ryan was completely confused by that. But he knew better than to question his father any further.

* * *

Ryan had a more hardscrabble upbringing than most Pennington kids. His parents split up when Ryan was four and his sister was six. Mae, his mother, kept the family's two-story duplex in Pennington following the divorce while his father moved to Manchester. Neither Darren nor Mae remarried. Mae had a couple of different live-in boyfriends while Ryan was growing up, neither of whom he could stand. Ryan saw the occasional girlfriend at his father's apartment, though he was seldom introduced to them, and none of them seemed to last very long. The Cunningham children lived with their mother. Ryan spent every other weekend with his father; his sister sometimes accompanied him and sometimes did not.

    Mae was a hairdresser, working at a beauty salon in Pennington center. She worked in the same place throughout Ryan's childhood, keeping her job through both good and bad economic times, though her hours typically suffered whenever the economy did. In her mind, she did her best to be a good mother. But earning a living and keeping a boyfriend happy often left little time for her kids.

    Ryan was never sure what his father did. He knew that for a while, Darren worked nights at a Budweiser distributorship, stocking the trucks that delivered Buds to bars and liquor stores in southern New Hampshire. Darren also sometimes tended bar at a Chili's in Manchester that Ryan occasionally went to with his mother and sister. But he also heard conflicting stories from his mother and father that he found hard to sort out. On more than one occasion, his father told him—and Mae—that he'd been laid off. But Mae never seemed to believe him; she would tell Ryan that it wasn't true, that his father was just using that as an excuse for not making child-support payments.

In reality, Darren's primary occupation was working as a bookie. He did work part-time at the Budweiser distributorship, but that was primarily to establish a source of income that he could report on his tax returns. He certainly wasn't going to report bookmaking income to the IRS. And he knew that if he reported no income but had money to spend on things like rent and car payments, he'd run into trouble sooner or later—if not from the IRS then from his ex-wife. He also worked a few bartending shifts each week at Chili's, where he knew the owner. That was an especially sweet gig. First, he got paid in cash, off the books, which wasn't taken into account by the court in determining the amount of his child-support payments. Second, his bartending customers were a great source of bookmaking business.

Darren had been betting on sporting events since his early twenties. He didn't regard himself as having a gambling problem—he didn't bet on a daily basis, never bet large amounts, and was always able to pay off his losses. But he did have a gambling problem in one sense: Like the vast majority of regular bettors, over time, despite the occasional big win, he lost more money than he won. It took him over ten years to come to this realization, but it eventually dawned on Darren that it would be more lucrative to take the bets than to place them.

The bookie Darren bet with, a guy named Petey, was a friend of Darren's older brother, and Darren knew him pretty well. For about two years, Darren peppered Petey with questions about the bookmaking business and how he could get into it. Petey continually rebuffed him, concerned that, given the number of people they knew in common, any bets Darren took would eat into Petey's business. One day, however, Petey approached Darren with a proposal. Petey's live-in girlfriend wanted to move to Florida to be closer to her mother, who had recently suffered a stroke. After a lifetime of frigid New Hampshire winters and cold, wet springs, that sounded pretty good to Petey. So he told Darren he would sell him his bookie business for $25,000.

As anxious as Darren was to get into the business, he couldn't quite figure out what he'd be paying $25,000 for. In his mind, to be a bookie, you needed a cell phone, access to people who liked to bet, and some balls. He didn't need to get any of that from Petey. But after a few conversations, Petey convinced him that he had two things of value Darren should be willing to pay for: a list of active clients and a business arrangement with a gentleman higher on the bookmaking food chain. Darren and Petey eventually struck a deal whereby Darren would pay him $15,000 for his business: $7,500 now (which, with some effort, Darren was able to scrounge together after about three weeks) and $7,500 over the next six months.

Darren made a halfway decent living as a bookie. He was what's known as an "independent" bookie. That is, he was in business for himself, and he paid off the bets he took out of the betting money he received. That was financially riskier than simply collecting commissions for taking bets on behalf of another party who was responsible for paying off the winners. But it was—at least in theory—more profitable. And being his own boss appealed to both Darren's independent streak and his indolence.

    For any bookie, the key to making money is a reliable point spread and a steady stream of bets. Darren took bets mostly on NFL, NBA, college football, and college basketball games. Every game had a point spread—the number of points by which the favored team was expected to win. Suppose Alabama's football team was favored by seven points over LSU. If you bet on Alabama, Alabama had to win by more than seven points for you to win your bet. Conversely, a bet on LSU would pay off if LSU either won the game or lost by fewer than seven points. The purpose of point spreads—which were set by Las Vegas oddsmakers and used by bookies all over the world—was to ensure that relatively even amounts were bet on both teams. It didn't always work out that way; sometimes Darren took in much more money on one team, particularly if local teams were involved. In those situations Darren stood to either win or lose a fair amount of money, depending on who won. Such was the case with the Patriots-Jets game, when the heavy betting on the hometown Patriots would have forced Darren to pay thousands of dollars in winnings out of his own pocket if the Patriots had beat the spread. With a fair point spread, though, roughly the same amount was usually bet on each team—meaning that no matter who won, Darren could pay off the winners out of the bets he collected and make his money on his commission rather than on the outcome of the game.

All bookies had methods of collecting commissions on the bets they took. Darren used a system whereby you had to risk $11 to win $10. For example, to win $100 if Alabama beat LSU (after factoring in the point spread), you had to put up $110 with Darren. If Alabama won, you got your $110 back plus $100 in winnings; if Alabama lost, you forfeited your $110. That 10 percent spread between what Darren took in on a losing bet and what he paid out on a winning bet was the primary source of his earnings.

Though Darren was in business for himself, he did have a boss in some sense. Just like Petey, Darren paid 10 percent of his profits as tribute to a shady figure known to Darren only as Dom. His only contact with Dom was a monthly meeting in a Manchester bar. Darren assumed the guy was connected to organized crime, but he didn't know how deep or how high his ties were. In exchange for Darren's payments, Dom supposedly made sure the Manchester cops left Darren alone and that no one else strong-armed Darren for a cut of his earnings. Darren never knew for certain whether Dom actually did that; after all, just because Darren hadn't been hassled by the cops or other wise guys didn't necessarily mean that was the result of Dom's auspices.

When Darren made his deal with Petey, he had pressed Petey on whether he really needed to give Dom a 10 percent cut. Petey had replied, "Listen to me. Always pay him, and don't ever shortchange him."

Darren had laughed nervously. "What would happen if I did?"

Petey had grown dead serious. "You don't want to know. Trust me on this."

Darren took that warning to heart and, despite his doubts on whether he was really getting anything for it, always paid Dom in full and on time. Darren never had any problems with mobsters or other bookies. That would not turn out to be the case for his son Ryan.

Chapter 5

Just before nine o'clock on a Saturday evening in October, nine-year-old Nick Sullivan was sitting in his basement, his attention divided between a college football game on ESPN and his Nintendo Game Boy. Hearing his father's footsteps coming down the stairs, he turned off his Game Boy and lowered the volume on the TV.

Matt perched on the arm of the couch Nick was sitting on. "I think it's about time for you to be getting to bed."

"What time is it?" asked Nick.

"About nine. But you have to get up awfully early tomorrow."

"What time?"

"Four fifteen. Four thirty at the latest."

Nick laughed. "Really?"

"Well, your game's at six. But you have to be there by five thirty. And Exeter's about a forty-five-minute ride from here, so we have to leave by quarter to five. So, yeah, I'd say four fifteen. Leave you time to get out of bed and get a quick bite to eat."

"Is it even light out then?"

"Been a long time since I was up at that hour, so I'm not sure. But probably not."

"How 'bout if I go to bed at ten? I won't be tired."

"You might not feel sleepy tired. But you need to be rested. This is your first game with the Catamounts. You wanna be at your best."

"If I go to bed now, can I play Game Boy in bed for a while?"

"OK—but lights out at nine thirty. I'll be up to check."

After Nick went up to bed, Matt went into the family room and sat down on the couch next to his wife, contemplating both his own bedtime and the hockey experience Nick—and his parents—were embarking upon. For the prior three years, Nick had played on the Pennington Mite A team, which was a fairly family-friendly program. They played on weekend mornings but never earlier than seven thirty. They traveled to other towns but never farther than about twenty miles. The Mite As had been a terrific experience for Nick, and his love for hockey really blossomed. During his last two years on the team, he got to play with Owen and Ryan. And he really excelled on the ice. Playing mostly center, he led his team in goals all three years (even though no official statistics were supposed to be kept, one of the assistant coaches tallied the players' goal scoring, and Chris made sure to get frequent updates on those stats). By his third year in the program, it was obvious even to a casual observer that Nick was far superior to any other player in the league. Following that season, at the suggestion of both his Mite coach and the president of Pennington

Youth Hockey, Nick tried out for—and made—the Manchester Catamounts.

The Catamounts were one of the area's "select" teams, which were just beginning to proliferate in New England in the 1990s. Select teams were different from town teams in many respects. They could draw players from anywhere, not just a single town. Whereas there was always a spot on one of the town teams for any kid who wanted to play hockey, select teams cut most of the kids who tried out for them; some of the better teams often had seventy-five to one hundred kids competing for about sixteen spots. This was the primary draw of select teams—playing with better players against better competition. Select teams were also distinguished by a number of other factors: a longer season, games at all kinds of crazy hours, travel all over New England (and sometimes into New York), and more pressure on the players to win. These could all be viewed as positives or negatives, depending on your point of view. Matt's perspective could best be described as skeptical.

"Do you want me to take Nick tomorrow, or would you rather go?" Matt asked Chris. One of them had to stay home with Nick's younger sisters. Matt enjoyed watching Nick play, but he was half hoping that Chris would spare him from a 4:00 a.m. alarm.

"Doesn't matter. I'll go if you don't want to."

"No, it's fine; I want to go." Matt paused. "I hope this is all worth it. This isn't going to be easy on him or us."

"Well, you know what we told him last week when we got the schedule. The first time we go in to wake him up early and he doesn't want to get out of bed, we let him stay in bed. But that's it—he's done with hockey from then on."

That was in fact exactly what they'd said to Nick; more precisely, what Matt had said to Nick. Chris had nodded in assent, but she wasn't sure she meant it. She already had high aspirations for Nick as a hockey player, and she didn't want those thrown away based on a single instance of a nine-year-old having a hard time getting out of bed before sunrise. She went along with the message only because she viewed it as a good way of testing Nick's mettle. In her mind, Nick's achieving success at hockey—whether that meant a productive high-school career, the chance to play college hockey, or something more—required both natural athletic ability and a tremendous resolve to succeed. She had already seen pretty good evidence of the former. Things like a 4:15 a.m. wake-up would serve as a good measuring stick of the latter.

Matt's clock-radio clicked on at four o'clock the next morning. He turned it off quickly so as not to awaken Chris. He spent ten minutes in the bathroom, got dressed, and then walked quietly down the hall to awaken Nick. Opening the door to Nick's room, he was astonished to see Nick sitting on his bed, wide awake and fully dressed, with a big smile on his face.

* * *

Dante—unlike Nick, Owen, and Ryan—did not play hockey. Youth hockey was, in general, an expensive proposition that demanded a lot of commitment not only from the players but also from their parents. Much to Dante's disappointment, Dante's father, Anthony, quickly concluded that youth hockey would be too taxing on his finances and his time. In reality, Pennington Youth Hockey offered reduced tuition to families when it was warranted by financial circumstances, and Dante's friends could have easily provided rides to practices and games. But Anthony hadn't bothered to look into any of that; saying no was quicker and easier.

Anthony Lombardo was regarded by Dante's friends as something of a hard-ass. Dante's mother had died several years earlier, and since her death his father's personality had taken on a darker edge. On more than one occasion when Dante's friends were over, they had witnessed his father verbally berate Dante for seemingly no reason. Several of Dante's friends suspected his father drank a lot, and a few also believed he hit Dante, although none of them had ever seen that. Dante's one sibling, a brother six years his senior, was away in the army, so Dante was left to bear the impact of his volatile father on his own.

Even though he wasn't playing hockey with them, Dante spent a lot of time with his three friends. At least two of them always seemed to be in his classes at school, and all four of them played several years of youth football, baseball, and lacrosse together. Dante was well liked by not only his peers but also his coaches and teachers, who regarded him as a hardworking, dependable kid.

Sensing that his homelife was less than ideal, Nick's parents and Owen's parents made a real effort to include Dante in things like going out to eat or taking in a movie, and Dante frequently slept over at their houses on weekends. Many kids his age would take for granted the hospitality extended by their friends' families. Dante, however, did not. He realized that he was doing things and receiving attention that he would not experience at home, and he was very appreciative of that.

Dante was not as athletic as Nick, as smart as Owen, or as adventurous as Ryan. But he was a loyal and considerate kid who would do anything for the other boys. He seemed to value their friendship a little more than the others did, maybe because he needed it more than they did.

* * *

By the time Nick was an eighth grader, his reputation as a phenomenal player was well established in New England hockey circles. Still, Matt and Chris were surprised to find Nick being recruited by a number of different high schools. It wasn't that they had reservations about whether he was good enough to warrant that attention; it was just that they didn't even realize high schools engaged in athletic recruiting.

Not all high schools recruit, of course. Public high schools can enroll only students living within the town or region served by the school. Private schools, such as Catholic high schools or prep schools, however, are bound by no such geographic constraint. In addition, many private high schools are blessed with endowments that enable them to offer scholarships to athletic or academic standouts.

During the course of eighth grade, Nick was contacted by eight prep schools spread all over New England as well as a handful of Catholic schools. Nick and his parents made two decisions early in the process that helped narrow down his options. First, Nick would attend either a Catholic or a prep school because the quality of hockey play was higher there than it was at most public high schools. Second, he would not board at a school, which eliminated many of the prep schools that were wooing him. Nick had no desire to live away from home, and his parents did not believe he was ready to do so; besides, there were plenty of attractive options within the area. By the time spring rolled around, Nick and his parents had winnowed their alternatives down to two possibilities: St. Xavier, located in Pennington, and Windsor Academy, situated just north of the Massachusetts state line and about a twenty-minute ride from the Sullivan home.

Nick really liked the hockey coach at Windsor, and he and his parents had been dazzled by Windsor's first-class facilities and opulent campus. Ultimately, though, Nick strongly preferred St. Xavier, primarily for two reasons: Owen, Dante, and Ryan would all be attending St. Xavier; and, unlike Windsor and the two other local Catholic schools that had been recruiting him, St. Xavier was coed. Nick had the good sense to soft-pedal those two factors in explaining his preference to his parents. Matt and Chris needed little convincing, though. They liked St. Xavier as well and fully supported Nick's choice.

Chapter 6

Owen turned the corner onto his street, hunched over the handlebars of his ten-speed bike, pumping hard. He was riding home from Pennington Middle School, which all four Anderson children attended. Owen was an eighth grader, his twin sisters were in sixth grade, and his brother was a fifth grader. He liked to get home from school at least five minutes before his younger siblings, which was why he rode his bike while they took the bus.

He entered the house through the door leading from the garage to the kitchen. Finding the kitchen empty, he checked the living room and the family room. No one. His mother's car was in the garage, which meant she was probably upstairs in her bedroom.

Owen knocked softly on the door to his parents' bedroom and then slowly pushed it open. His mother was lying in bed, on top of the covers, snoring softly. A glass was spilled on the nightstand, the ice cubes not yet melted. A mostly empty pint of vodka was on the floor next to the bed.

* * *

Bridget Anderson, now forty-one, had never drunk much before she reached her late thirties. She had been exposed to drinking growing up, but that made her less rather than more inclined to drink herself. Her parents and aunts and uncles always drank at holiday get-togethers and other family functions, and invariably one (or more) of them ended up saying or doing something stupid. Bridget was put off by that and, save for an occasional glass of wine when she went out to dinner, steered clear of alcohol—even during her college days.

    She started drinking about a year after her youngest child, Michael, entered first grade. Increasingly bored and restless during the day, with all four kids in school until midafternoon, she found herself looking for diversions. One day she went to lunch in Manchester with two childhood friends who no longer lived in Pennington and whom Bridget saw only sporadically. When both of her friends ordered wine with lunch, Bridget thought, *What the hell*, and did the same. The overdue lunch among friends who hadn't seen each other in a while stretched into a two-and-a-half-hour affair, and many glasses of wine were consumed. Bridget returned home with a smile on her face and a glow in her head, watched some TV, did a little reading, and enjoyed her afternoon for the first time in months.

    About a week later, Bridget bought a bottle of wine while she was out doing some morning errands. Intending to enjoy a glass or two with her lunch, she ended up polishing off most of the bottle by midafternoon. She once again liked the way it made her feel—the TV shows she watched seemed funnier, the music she listened to sounded richer, and her mood was brighter. When the kids got home from school, even though she was tipsy and her speech was slightly slurred, only Owen—then ten—

noticed that something was different about her. But he wasn't old enough yet to realize that she was drunk.

From that point forward, drinking during the afternoon became a regular part of Bridget's routine. It wasn't an everyday event. Bridget was still a loving and, for the most part, responsible mother and active in town affairs. Once or twice a week, however, she'd surrender to the temptation and start drinking—usually to excess—around noon.

Bridget would almost always stop drinking when the kids got home from school—partly because of maternal guilt, partly because it was hard to sneak drinks with four kids running around, and occasionally because she was passed out by then—so she was generally sober, or at least coherent, when Mark got home from work between six and seven o'clock. As a result, it was several months before Mark discovered her daytime drinking. Hints began to emerge—Bridget sometimes tripped over her words during dinner, Mark occasionally found an empty liquor bottle in the trash, Bridget was no longer reticent to order drinks when they went out—and Mark eventually confronted her about it.

Bridget had anticipated this and was prepared for it. She had decided that her best response was neither a staunch denial nor a tearful confession but rather something that bisected those two bookends. She told Mark that yes, she occasionally had a couple of drinks during the afternoon, but it was only an every-other-week-or-so occurrence, she usually did it with friends, and she was careful to not let it interfere with her family duties.

Mark didn't know whether to buy that or not. They had a strong marriage; he had never seen her truly drunk, and nothing in the twenty-five years he'd known her pointed to this being a problem for her. As a lawyer, though, he was used to being fed stories and excuses, and he was naturally inclined to be skeptical about what he was hearing from Bridget. He decided to enlist the aid of Owen, whom Mark considered to be unusually mature and responsible for his age. One night Mark sat Owen down and told him that his mother sometimes had a few drinks during the day. He told Owen that she was still a good mother, and her drinking usually wasn't a problem, but Owen should be watchful just in case she ever got to the point where she was actually drunk.

"I'm not asking you to spy on her or tell me if she's drinking," Mark told him. "I just want you to keep an eye on the other kids if it's ever the case that your mother isn't able to."

Owen was fairly surprised, and also confused, about the whole situation. Lots of questions ran through his head: *Why is she drinking? How will I know if she's drunk? What do drunk people act like?* But he had no doubt that he'd figure things out and be able to do what his father asked of him.

* * *

Pennington didn't really have any "bad" sections of town, but the area where Ryan grew up was a relatively tough neighborhood. Known as The Falls, it was located just across the Merrimack River from Holbrook. Whereas Pennington was, in general, a prosperous town, Holbrook had fallen on hard times. For much of the twentieth century, Holbrook had been a thriving mill city of close to fifty thousand residents. Most of the town's jobs (and tax revenues) came from the textile and paper mills lining the Merrimack River. Beginning in the 1960s, however, advances in factory automation and cheaper offshore labor eroded the city's economy. By 1980 only one Holbrook mill remained operational, and it closed in 1988. Unemployment in the city by that point exceeded 20 percent.

Holbrook's demographics changed along with its economy's deterioration. By the time Ryan was born in 1986, the number of Holbrook residents had fallen to about twenty-five thousand. And close to half of the population was then comprised of Puerto Rican and Dominican immigrants and their descendants, who originally came to the city to find work in the mills and were later lured there by cheaper housing.

An inevitable by-product of high unemployment and a declining tax base to fund the city's schools and police force was a rise in crime. Drugs were rampant in Holbrook, with crack houses strewn throughout the city and many neighborhoods serving as open-air drug bazaars; prostitutes plied their trade with impunity; and many residents did not feel safe walking the streets at night.

Some of the blighted housing and crime plaguing Holbrook spread across the Miller Bridge into The Falls section of Pennington. Although that neighborhood was physically and economically a cut above Holbrook, there were plenty of opportunities for kids growing up in The Falls to find their way into trouble. Ryan did better than most in navigating the area's pitfalls, but he was not untainted by its vices.

Although Nick, Owen, and Dante were always his closest friends, it was natural for Ryan to also hang out with some kids from his neighborhood. The elementary school in The Falls had three outdoor basketball courts, lined on one side by aluminum bleachers. Ryan and a few other kids spent a fair bit of time at those courts. By the time he was in eighth grade, they were spending less time playing basketball and more time smoking pot in the bleachers. It was on those same bleachers where, as a high-school freshman, Ryan tried cocaine for the first time (although he used that drug again only a handful of times during high school). It also was not unheard of for Ryan and his Falls crew to engage in some shoplifting and small-time vandalism from time to time.

Ryan's pot smoking never became frequent enough to interfere with school or sports, and he never used drugs in front of Nick, Owen, or Dante. The other three, though, were not blind to the fact that Ryan sometimes crossed lines that they were not comfortable breaching.

News, both fact and rumor, travels quickly among high-school kids. Whether it's burgeoning romances, upcoming parties, or sexual conquests, secrets are hard to keep. Ryan's dark side, however, had no impact on their friendship. All three of the others played sports with Ryan and liked his fiery competitiveness, the way he wouldn't back down from anyone. They shared many of the same interests as Ryan and found him to be engaging and funny. Even his occasional reckless behavior gave him a certain cachet among kids who weren't willing to do some of the things that Ryan did. Adolescents seldom realize, though, that some of the traits that make a teenager "cool" can create real problems in adulthood.

* * *

After cleaning up the spilled glass next to his mother's bed, Owen returned the vodka bottle to the cupboard above the kitchen sink. He grabbed a blanket from the hallway closet, covered his mother up, and then closed the door. He was just coming downstairs when his sisters and brother got home from school.

His sisters were arguing over something. Seeing Owen, Kelly asked, "Is Mom home?"

"Yeah, but she's not feeling good. She's taking a nap."

"Can I wake her up? I need her to take me to the store."

"Just let her sleep for a while," Owen replied. "What do you need at the store?"

Kelly was annoyed. "I have to work on a project for social studies, making a map. I need to get this, like, extra-big construction paper. Plus I need some magic markers."

"We have a bunch of magic markers in the closet in the basement. Just use those. And we can get your paper at Staples."

"Who's gonna take me to Staples if I can't wake Mom up?"

"We'll take our bikes—it's not far."

"You're coming with me?"

"Yeah, let's go."

Before leaving, Owen tracked down his other sister and brother, who were watching TV in the basement, and reminded them not to disturb their mother.

"How come Mom's sick so much?" asked Kara.

"I think she's got allergies of some kind. They make her sick to her stomach and really sleepy." Owen paid careful attention to their reactions, but neither showed any interest in pursuing it. Relieved, he headed upstairs to go to Staples with Kelly.

4th of July, Kingsbridge Park

Chapter 7

Bzzzzzzzzt.

Bzzzzzzzzt.

Eighteen-year-old Ryan Cunningham heard the doorbell ringing. He dragged himself off his living room couch and started heading toward the front door, but he was having trouble getting there. It was inexplicably foggy inside the house, and he was struggling to find the door.

Bzzzzzzzzt.

He stumbled forward in the murky haze and reached toward where he was sure the front door was. But it was a closet door he jerked open instead.

Bzzzzzzzzt.

Now he was completely disoriented. He felt his way along the wall, moving to his left, fumbling for the doorknob. But every time he thought it was within his reach, it somehow eluded his grasp.

Bzzzzzzzzt.

Ryan's dream ended as he awoke with a start to the buzzing of his cell phone on the nightstand next to his bed. It was 10:19 on the morning of Saturday, July 3.

Ryan flipped the phone open. "Hello," he mumbled.

"What's up, man? You weren't sleeping, were you?" The voice of Dante Lombardo crackled through phone.

"Whatever. What's going on?"

"You hear about the party at Winnipesaukee tomorrow night? At Kirby Nolan's parents' house?"

"I don't even like that guy."

"Who cares?" Dante said. "It's a Fourth of July party! It'll be fun."

Ryan and Dante, along with Nick, Owen, and 513 of their classmates, had graduated from St. Xavier High School about a month earlier. It wouldn't be long before their group of friends would start to disperse, with most heading off to college, some joining the armed services, and a few entering the workforce. Though most of the group held down summer jobs, they were doing their best to enjoy what might be their last summer together. Sunday was the Fourth of July, making it a great day for a party. The fact that some of the kids also had that Monday off made it even better.

"What, is Nolan's mom gonna put up balloons and serve cake to all his lame-ass friends?" asked Ryan.

"No, man, here's the deal," Dante said, excitement evident in his voice. "Nolan's parents told him he and a few of his friends could stay over at their lake house Sunday night, as long as his older sister was there, too. But I guess she told Kirby that he could have as many friends as he wanted up there; she didn't care."

"Who's his sister?"

"I don't know, she's like twenty-two or twenty-six or something. What the fuck difference does it make? A ton of people are going."

"Girls too?"

"Yeah. I heard, like Scanlon, Beauregard, and all those girls are going. And pretty much the whole soccer team."

"That sounds pretty cool." Ryan paused. "So your dad gonna let you go?"

"Yeah. Listen, I told him we were going camping—me, you, Owen, and Sully—up at Winnipesaukee. He doesn't know anything about Nolan's house."

"Alright, that'll work for me. My mom won't give a shit. You talk to Sully and Owen yet?"

"I talked to Owen this morning," replied Dante. "He's the one that told me about the party. I just tried calling Nick but he didn't pick up."

"You wanna get something to eat in a little while? We can try and hook up with Nick and Owen then."

"Yeah, sure. Oh, wait a minute—I bet Sully won't be able to go! Doesn't he leave on Monday?"

"Oh, fuck, that's right," exclaimed Ryan. "But he should still be able to go. We can be home Monday morning."

"I don't know, man. I bet he has to get ready and shit."

"Man, it'd suck if the four of us can't get together like that one more time before he leaves."

After a brief pause, Dante said, "We gotta talk to Owen. If anyone can get Sully to come, it's Owen."

Chapter 8

Dante pulled his Honda Civic into the Andersons' driveway shortly before noon on Saturday. Ryan was riding shotgun. Not ten seconds after Dante beeped the horn, Owen emerged from his house and pulled open the passenger door.

"You want me to jump in back?" asked Ryan.

"No, I got it," Owen replied. As Ryan leaned forward, Owen squeezed into the back seat.

The car, which Dante had bought from his older brother for $500, was pushing 150,000 miles. It was pretty beat up, although the tears and stains on the interior were largely obscured by the scattered fast-food bags, empty soda cans, and sweatshirts. None of the boys minded, though. Among the four of them, only Dante owned a car. Although Nick and Owen were occasionally able to borrow their parents' cars, Dante was the only dependable source of transportation for social outings—particularly an overnight excursion.

"So where we going to eat?" asked Owen.

Dante shrugged. "I don't know. Where you guys feel like going?"

"I don't care," said Ryan, looking out the side window.

"How about Taco Bell?" offered Owen.

After mumbles of assent from both of the front-seat passengers, Ryan turned around to look at Owen and asked, "So, you talk to Sully about Winnipesaukee?"

"Yeah, I talked to him last night and then again this morning. He asked his parents about it last night and I guess they said no at first. He kept pushing it, though, and finally his father said he'd think about it some more. They're supposed to let him know this afternoon."

"What the hell, man." Ryan was irritated. "We're going, like, tomorrow. When's he gonna fucking decide?"

"What's the difference?" Owen's tone was relaxed, not challenging. "The three of us are going for sure. If Nick can come, great. If he can't, we'll still go. It's not like we need to know what Sully's doing to make our own plans."

Ryan wasn't satisfied. "Well, we gotta figure out how much beer we're gonna get."

"What's the deal with that?" asked Dante. "You nail that down with Heather yet?" Heather was Ryan's girlfriend.

"Yeah, we're all set," said Ryan, smiling. "Her sister's going to buy the beer for us tonight and keep it in her trunk. We just gotta pick it up sometime tomorrow before we leave."

"Great," said Owen. "We'll know by tonight whether Sully's coming. Then you can tell her how much to get."

* * *

Nick spent a good part of Saturday either packing his things or running to CVS and Walmart to pick up items he realized he needed only during the course of packing.

His flight was early Monday afternoon. As—hopefully—he'd be up at Lake Winnipesaukee from midday Sunday until early Monday, he wanted to get as much done on Saturday as he could. Two almost-full duffel bags lay on his bedroom floor. One contained clothes, toiletries, and other odds and ends; the second held his hockey gear.

Nick had been picked near the end of the first round in the National Hockey League entry draft held two weeks earlier. In the annual NHL draft, all thirty teams take turns selecting amateur players from around the world. Players can be chosen from the college ranks, junior hockey leagues (competitive leagues in which post-high-school players prepare for college or pro hockey), European leagues, and high schools and prep schools. Around the time Nick was selected, Americans constituted a distinct minority of the players selected, and less than 5 percent of all players drafted were US high-school players.

A smooth-skating, strong defenseman, Nick had built an impressive résumé by the time he'd finished high school. He was a three-time all-state selection, garnering player of the year honors in New Hampshire in both his junior and senior seasons, and he had played on the US team that won the gold medal at the under-eighteen world championships held in Belarus during the spring of his senior year. Leading up to the NHL draft, Nick had been ranked by various scouting services as anywhere from the number twenty-nine to the number forty-seven prospect in the draft. So Nick and his parents were confident he would be drafted, but there remained a lot of uncertainty about how high he'd be drafted. His selection in the first round was exciting for both its financial implications and for what it said about his prospects in the league.

In addition to being thrilled about where he was drafted, Nick was delighted about who drafted him—the Detroit Red Wings. One of the "original six" NHL teams, the Red Wings were one of the most popular and successful organizations in the sport, having won three Stanley Cup championships in the preceding ten years. His parents were also pleased with the fact that Detroit was about a two-hour flight from Manchester—much closer than some other NHL cities, such as Edmonton or San Jose.

The vast majority of players drafted directly out of US high schools do not play in the NHL right away; most spend at least a year or two in junior hockey, college, or the minor leagues. Nick was very cognizant of that fact and was trying hard to manage his expectations. On the other hand, he was well aware that Detroit had lost two defensemen to free agency since the end of the season, and there appeared to be room for at least one rookie defenseman to make the team. The Red Wings' rookie camp, which began on Tuesday morning in suburban Detroit, was the first step in his quest to be that player.

Downstairs, Matt and Chris were discussing whether to let Nick go to Lake Winnipesaukee with his friends. Chris was against it. She believed he should be focusing on the upcoming camp, and she harbored a nagging uneasiness about the prospect of getting into trouble up there, largely because she didn't completely trust Ryan. Matt, more laid back than Chris, understood his son's desire to have one more get-together with his friends before going away and was OK with the trip. When Matt and Chris disagreed on something, it was more often than not resolved in Chris's favor, because she usually felt more fervently about the matter, and Matt had learned long ago to pick his battles. But Matt could sense that Nick was a little bit stressed about rookie camp and thought this overnighter with his friends would be good for his psyche. So he held his ground, and Chris eventually gave in. They then both went upstairs to deliver the news to Nick.

Nick's first call was to Owen. Owen then called Ryan to finalize their beer order.

Chapter 9

It was two o'clock on Sunday afternoon. Dante's Civic was cruising up Route 93, the primary highway running north and south through New Hampshire, heading for Lake Winnipesaukee—more precisely, for Kingsbridge Park, where the Nolans' house was located. Owen was in the front passenger seat, with Nick and Ryan crammed in the back. The trunk held four sleeping bags, four backpacks containing a change of clothes and some toiletries, and a cooler with a case of Pabst Blue Ribbon on ice. The temperature was pushing ninety degrees, and the boys' spirits were high.

"So how many people you think are gonna be here?" asked Dante.

"Just about everyone I talked to is going," replied Nick. "I think this is gonna be a good time."

"Yeah, I called Kirby this morning to get directions," said Owen. "He said he invited fifty or sixty kids. Guys and girls."

"But they won't all show, right?" Ryan chimed in. "So maybe there'll only be, like, thirty people."

Owen laughed. "No way, man, you know how it works. Not everyone Kirby talked to will come. But there will be a bunch of kids he didn't ask that show up anyway."

"Plus, I bet some of his sister's friends'll be there," Dante said excitedly. "That'd be pretty sweet."

"Yeah, like those older chicks are gonna give us the fuckin' time of day," Ryan replied.

"Chill, Ryan," said Dante, grinning. "Sully's a Goddamn celebrity. They're gonna be all over his ass."

"Hey, brother," Ryan said, playfully backhanding Nick in the stomach. "You better spread the wealth."

"Look, man, I got a long day ahead of me tomorrow," replied Nick. "I just wanna kick back, maybe have a couple of beers, and lay low."

* * *

Kingsbridge Park, New Hampshire, was perched on the southwestern edge of Lake Winnipesaukee, about seven miles off Route 93. Kingsbridge Park was a town of less than three thousand people, although its population usually swelled by over fifteen hundred during the summer months. The center of town consisted of little more than a post office, a general store (which sold everything from food and beer to inflatable rafts), and a combination town hall/police station/fire station that barely looked large enough to house even one of those functions.

The Nolans' house was on Lakeview Drive, a two-lane road that snaked its way for five miles along the edge of Lake Winnipesaukee. In some places the road hugged the shoreline, offering magnificent views of the lake to the stately, well-tended homes along the route. Other parts of the road meandered into the woods, up to half a mile away from the lake. The dwellings along the stretches of Lakeview Drive where there wasn't actually a lake view tended to be smaller, consisting mostly of two- and three-bedroom cottages, many of which were not winterized. The Nolan residence, a four-bedroom house located about a quarter of a mile off the water, was one of the nicer places on that stretch of the road.

When the Civic pulled up to the house a little before three o'clock, there were already close to twenty cars parked in the driveway, along the road, and even on parts of the front lawn.

"Should we grab our stuff now?" asked Nick, unfolding his body from the backseat.

"Let's leave it for now till we figure out where we're gonna put it," replied Owen.

"Fine, but I'm bringing the cooler," said Ryan. "Dante, pop the trunk?"

"Yeah, sure. I'll give you a hand."

"Nah, I got it."

Bypassing the front door, the boys followed the sound of voices and music around to the back of the house. There they found about forty people, some clustered on a wooden deck jutting off the back the house, others hanging out in a fairly spacious backyard. Some of the kids were playing Wiffle ball, many were drinking beer, and a few were dancing on the deck. Pretty much everyone looked to be having a good time.

"Yo, Kirby, what's up, man?" yelled Owen as they rounded the corner into the backyard.

"Hey, guys, how you doin'? You find the place alright?" Kirby was holding court on the deck.

"Yeah, no problem," replied Dante. "I just turned where Owen told me to turn."

Dante and Owen headed up onto the deck to greet Kirby. Nick was intercepted by two girls before he even reached the deck. Ryan used that as an excuse to plop the cooler down on the ground, stopping next to Nick.

"Hey, Hannah, Stacy. You guys want a beer?"

Hannah and Stacy exchanged a quick glance. "No, I'm good," replied Hannah, as Stacy shook her head.

Ryan grabbed two beers out of the cooler, handing one to Nick and cracking open the other. Nick hesitated before opening his beer. His rational mind was telling him that he shouldn't drink or risk getting into trouble with training camp looming. But he was also hearing whispers that he'd been training hard all summer, that this was the last time in who knew how long that he'd be out with his friends, and that drinking once this summer wouldn't hurt. He popped the tab on his can of PBR.

*　*　*

To the immediate northwest of Kingsbridge Park stood Wachovia, another small lakeside town. Wachovia was known for two things. The first was Leeds Beach, a village within Wachovia that featured an expansive, sandy beach along Lake Winnipesaukee and a honky-tonk beachside strip teeming with arcades, shops, and bars.

Wachovia's second claim to fame was Bike Week, a weeklong extravaganza held each July that attracted, over the course of the week, close to one hundred thousand visitors—most of them astride motorcycles. Among the attractions during Bike Week were motorcycle races, hill-climbing contests, and bike exhibitions. Bike Week had mellowed somewhat in recent years—public displays of both drunkenness and female breasts had become less frequent. But so-called outlaw bikers still represented a small minority of those in attendance. Satan's Knights were part of that element.

Loosely based in Manchester, Satan's Knights had members scattered around southern New Hampshire and northern Massachusetts. The number of active members generally ranged from twenty-five to thirty-five, and was affected primarily by relocations and incarcerations. Satan's Knights members held group barbeques, went on long rides together, and worked on each other's bikes. They also started bar fights, sold coke and meth, and ran prostitutes.

Wachovia Bike Week had begun the preceding weekend. Roughly fifteen Satan's Knights were planning to show up at various points during the week, but none of them had gotten around to reserving a cottage, motel rooms, or a campground site in Wachovia. With the influx of visitors taking up all available accommodations within Wachovia, they were forced to look to the surrounding towns. After a few days of fruitless efforts, one of the members found a cottage for rent in Kingsbridge Park. It was only three bedrooms, hardly enough to comfortably handle the ten to fifteen of them who would be staying there at any one time. But none of them minded crashing in a sleeping bag on the floor or back deck—especially because sleep generally came fairly easy after drinking beer and Wild Turkey all day.

The cottage also offered a few key benefits. Leeds Beach was only a few miles away. It was a short walk through the woods to the Lake Winnipesaukee shore. And, perhaps most importantly, there was little risk that any neighbors would complain about loud voices, loud music, or loud bikes: no house was visible to either side, and because the cottage was set back about fifty yards from the street, they didn't expect any trouble with the house directly across Lakeview Drive—the house owned by the Nolan family.

Chapter 10

By seven thirty Sunday evening, the party was in full swing. Close to seventy-five kids—all from St. Xavier—were now gathered at the Nolans' house. A number of kids were inside the house, mostly concentrated in the living room and kitchen, while others occupied the back deck, and still more were hanging out in the backyard. Kirby and Owen had collected a few bucks from most of the kids there and had just placed a delivery order for twelve pizzas. About half of the kids were drinking. A few kids had retreated to the woods behind the house to smoke some pot. From time to time a couple would disappear into an upstairs bedroom for a few minutes. As high-school parties go, it was about as good as it gets.

Dante and Ryan were in the backyard, talking with two girls. One was Heather, Ryan's girlfriend; the other was one of Heather's best friends, a pretty blonde named Samantha. Dante had always considered Samantha to be attractive and charming, and he viewed this as a perfect opportunity to pursue his interest in her. He wasn't making much progress with that, but he was enjoying himself nonetheless. Both he and Ryan were working on their fourth beers.

Inside the house Nick, Owen, Kirby, and five other guys were clustered around the TV in the living room, watching the Red Sox-Yankees game on ESPN. All of the kids there were big baseball fans, so there was lots of banter about the game, much of it humorous and some of it profane. One of the kids in the room, Tyler Rizzo, was a transplanted New Yorker and an ardent Yankees fan, which added a little spice to the chatter.

As Derek Jeter, the venerable shortstop and captain of the Yankees, stepped to the plate, Kirby exclaimed, "Jeter blows."

"C'mon, man, how can you rag on Jeter?" responded Tyler.

"Because he's a fuckin' Yankee, that's how."

"Help me out here, Owen. Jeter's a class act."

"Jeter's alright," Owen replied. "I can respect him, even if he is a Yankee. But I can't stand those giant blisters on his butt."

"What the hell you talking about—what blisters?" Tyler asked.

Nick picked up immediately on Owen's reference. "The blisters he has from everyone kissing his ass all the time," he responded with a laugh.

A bit later in the game, Jorge Posada, the Yankees catcher, drew a base on balls after a thirteen-pitch at-bat in which he fouled off nine pitches. "What a great at-bat by Posada," offered the ESPN play-by-play announcer.

"You're absolutely right, Dan," his announcing partner responded. "He really hung tough, fouling off a bunch of pitches with two strikes on him to draw that walk. Tremendous at-bat."

"I hate when announcers do that," said Owen.

"Do what?" Tyler asked.

"Say that a guy had a great at-bat just because he fouled off a lot of pitches. About nine times in a row, Posada tried to hit a pitch and he barely tipped it. What's so great about that? Last inning, Ortiz hit the first pitch he saw out of the park. You didn't hear anyone talking about what a great at-bat Ortiz had. But who had a better at-bat?"

"The answer is, 'Who the hell cares?'" Tyler replied.

"My point is, you can't always take everything you hear at face value."

Just then Ryan walked into the room, a mischievous grin on his face. A couple of minutes earlier, he had noticed his friend Kenny Allenson and his girlfriend leave the backyard together and head into the house. Ryan followed them into the house but didn't find them in any of the other first-floor rooms.

"Did Allenson and his girlfriend come through here a couple of minutes ago?"

"Yeah, I saw them head upstairs together," Nick replied.

"Kirby, you know which room they'd be in?" asked Ryan, still smiling.

"I told Kenny earlier to stay out of my parents' room and my sister's room with Liz. So he's probably in my room or the guest room."

Ryan quietly climbed a few steps up the stairs and saw three rooms with open doors and one closed door. He came back down, pointed at the closed door, and asked Kirby, "Is that your room at the top of the stairs to the right?"

"Yeah—why?" Kirby replied.

"No reason," said Ryan as he headed out the back door. He walked around to the front of the house and went into the garage, where he found a ladder. After walking along the right side of the house and locating the window for Kirby's room, Ryan leaned the ladder against the side of the house and began climbing it. By this time a small group of kids had gathered around the base of the ladder.

"What the hell you doing, Ryan?" one asked.

"You'll see," he said, grinning at the group as he ascended the rungs.

Kenny had had the good sense to shut the window and close the curtains in Kirby's bedroom before he and Liz got down to business. But there was a gap between the curtains through which Ryan could see the bottoms of four legs entangled on the bed. He started rapping on the window, softly at first but gradually increasing in force. The group below him had by now expanded to twelve kids.

After about sixty seconds, Kenny came to the window and pulled the curtain back just enough for him to peek out. He found himself about four inches from Ryan's grinning face. Bursting into laugher himself, Kenny raised the window, quickly removed the screen, and grabbed for Ryan. "You prick," he yelled, but he was still giggling. Ryan tried to dodge Kenny's flailing arms and almost fell off the ladder. The kids below were howling with laughter as Ryan tried to scramble down. He had gotten about halfway when Kenny shoved the top of the ladder away from the house. Feeling the ladder toppling backward, Ryan jumped off. His fall was broken by a few of the kids gathered below, and four of them tumbled to the ground, all laughing loudly.

As Ryan got to his feet, he heard Liz yell, "You asshole!" Looking up, he realized she was yelling not at him but at Kenny. He and the other kids below the window were now doubled over with laughter.

* * *

Just after eight o'clock that night, three St. Xavier boys were heading back to the Nolans' house after going for a quick swim in Lake Winnipesaukee. They were walking along the quarter-mile public walkway that began at the small community beach where they had been swimming and exited on Lakeview Drive about twenty yards from the Nolans' house—a walkway that skirted the edge of the property rented by the Satan's Knights. All three boys had been drinking beer since midafternoon, and they ranged from pleasantly buzzed to sloppily drunk.

About halfway between the beach and Lakeview Drive, the most inebriated of the group, Brett, said, "I gotta take a piss." Since the walkway was lighted, he ambled a few yards into the shrubs and undergrowth that lined the walkway. He was joined by a second kid, while the third, AJ, lingered on the walkway. AJ polished off the beer he had been drinking and tossed the bottle, aiming for a spot a few yards past the two kids relieving themselves. He was hoping to startle his two friends, but he drew an entirely different reaction.

Twenty yards from the public walkway, where the backyard of the rented cottage ended and the vegetation bordering the walkway began, a Satan's Knight named Tiny and his girlfriend were wrapped in a sleeping bag, in the throes of passion. Their lovemaking was interrupted when AJ's empty bottle thudded off Tiny's shoulder. It took Tiny a second to realize what had hit him. When he did, he scrambled to his feet, bellowing "Sonuvva fuckin' bitch!" Spotting the silhouettes of two figures in the brush, he ran toward them, clothed only in a T-shirt, with a pair of boxer shorts hanging off one of his ankles.

Seeing a half-naked, 250-pound figure crashing through the bushes toward them, the two boys quickly finished their business and ran back toward the walkway. When they emerged from the underbrush, all three boys started running in the direction of Lakeview Drive. After a few seconds, Brett looked back to check on the guy chasing them. By that time Tiny had run out of gas and was just standing in the middle of the walkway. With the safety of thirty yards between him and Tiny, Brett pulled up and called out to the other two boys to stop as well.

"You little fuckin' pricks! I see you again, I'm going beat the livin' shit out of all three of you!" shouted Tiny.

AJ, spooked by the whole incident and still walking backward away from Tiny, said to the other two, "Let's just get out of here."

Brett, fueled by liquid courage, wasn't quite ready to let it go. "Fuck you, you fat gorilla," he yelled. "Go find some fuckin' pants!" He then fired his empty beer bottle at Tiny. It exploded into shards about ten feet in front of the man. All three of the boys then took off running.

Tiny let out a roar and started running at the boys. His mindless charge lasted only a few seconds before he pulled up in pain, his left foot sliced by a piece of broken glass from Brett's bottle. "I'm gonna fuckin' kill you," he shrieked. "I'm gonna find you all and fuckin' kill you!"

By that time the three boys had reached Lakeview Drive, where they slowed to a walk as they approached the Nolans' house, rehashing the story among themselves. Brett had at first been eager to tell the story to the others at the party, no doubt embellishing it a bit more with each retelling. At AJ's urging, however, they all agreed to keep it to themselves (at least for now) so that Kirby didn't get pissed off and maybe kick them out of the party.

Chapter 11

Tiny stormed back toward the Satan's Knights' rented cottage, stopping at the yard's edge to put his clothes back on. His girlfriend had already dressed and was waiting for him at the sleeping bag. She didn't see the bottle hit Tiny and had no idea why he had suddenly jumped up and ran toward the walkway to the lake.

"What happened?" she asked.

"Shut the fuck up," he said. "Grab the fuckin' sleeping bag." He then walked ahead of her into the house, one foot still bare.

Five other guys were sitting in the kitchen when Tiny walked in, carrying one of his motorcycle boots. About twenty beer bottles, a bottle of Old Grand Dad whiskey, and a five-by-seven mirror covered the kitchen table. "What's up with you, man?" one of them asked Tiny.

Tiny explained what had happened.

"There's been a bunch of punk-ass kids walking up and down to the lake tonight," a biker named Vukie offered. "I bet they're coming from a party at one of the houses on this road."

"Yeah, well, the next kid I see coming down that path, I'm gonna rip him a new asshole," growled Tiny as he taped some gauze over the cut on the bottom of his left foot.

"That's what I like to hear, dude!" exclaimed Vukie, who was known for lots of talk and little action. "Let's kick their ass!"

"Fuck that, man," said another of the men seated in the kitchen. "You can't just beat the shit out of some random kid. The cops'll be swarming all over this place, and we'll all be fucked."

"Chill out, man," Tiny replied. "I'll make sure it's the same kids before I kick the living shit out of 'em. Now let's get some of that fuckin' crank goin'."

A skinny biker in his fifties took a vial out of the pocket of his Satan's Knights vest and poured two crystal-meth rocks out onto the mirror on the table. He broke them into smaller pieces with a pocketknife and then used a razor blade to chop them into a fine powder. The mirror with the crystal-meth powder was then passed around, making two round trips among the six Satan's Knights in the kitchen. Tiny vacuumed up the last line, shook his head violently as though he'd suffered an electrical shock, and shouted, "Those fuckin' kids are dead!"

* * *

Even at nine o'clock, with the sun down, it was a hot night. A few of the partygoers had made the ten-minute walk to the beach at Lake Winnipesaukee for a dip in the lake's cool waters, and Nick and Owen were about to follow suit. Neither was drunk, but they'd had a few beers each and were feeling a bit more uninhibited than they normally would.

"Let's see if Ryan and Dante wanna come," suggested Nick.

"OK. You seen those guys lately?" asked Owen.

"I think they're out back."

Nick and Owen found their two friends seated at a picnic table with Ryan's girlfriend Heather and Samantha, the girl Dante had been trying to talk to earlier that day without much success. His luck seemed to be improving, as Samantha was now laughing and talking animatedly with him.

"Hey, we're going down to the beach for a swim. We might watch the fireworks from down there too. Any of you guys feel like going?" asked Owen.

"Sounds good, man," Ryan said. "Where they shooting off fireworks from?"

"We heard they were having fireworks at Leeds Beach," replied Nick. "We oughta be able to see them pretty good from the beach."

"You girls up for it?" Ryan asked, turning to Heather and Samantha.

"I didn't bring a bathing suit," said Heather.

"I didn't either," Samantha chimed in.

"That's alright," said Ryan with a grin. "We can all go skinny-dipping."

"You're gross," Heather exclaimed, playfully whacking Ryan on his arm.

"Thanks, but I think I'll pass," said Samantha, pointedly ignoring Ryan and directing her response at Owen instead.

"Suit yourself, ladies," Ryan replied. "You don't know what you're missing. Dante, you in?"

Dante, sensing that he was making progress with Samantha, was in no hurry to leave. "After I finish this beer."

"Alright," Ryan said, turning back to Owen and Nick. "Me and Dante'll meet you guys down there in around fifteen, twenty minutes."

Nick and Owen both grabbed towels from their backpacks, walked the short stretch of Lakeshore Drive to the beginning of the walkway, and then headed down the walkway toward the beach. The beach was officially closed after the lifeguard went off duty at five o'clock, but it was frequently used after hours, especially by teenagers. There was no direct lighting there at night, but a streetlamp at the end of the walkway provided some faint illumination of the beach and the water's edge.

As Nick and Owen exited the walkway onto the beach, they noticed the silhouettes of two people sitting on the beach, facing the lake. Thinking it might be kids from the party, they walked toward the seated figures. Owen was wearing navy-blue gym shorts, a gray St. Xavier T-shirt, and a Red Sox hat. That happened to pretty much match the same outfit worn by the bottle-throwing Brett, who was also roughly the same height as Owen.

Tiny and Vukie were sharing a joint when they heard footsteps behind them. Tiny turned around to see the two boys approaching. Through the prism of eleven beers, multiple lines of meth, and a few joints, Tiny was sure he was looking at the kid who had cursed him out and tried to hit him with an empty beer bottle. Tiny jumped to his feet. Vukie did the same.

Nick and Owen had just gotten close enough to realize the two guys sitting on the beach were bikers, not classmates, when Tiny turned toward them. They had turned away and were heading for another area of the beach when Tiny bellowed, "Where the fuck do you think you pussies are going?"

The boys stopped and turned, about twenty-five feet from where Tiny and Vukie were standing. "Sorry, we thought you were someone else," said Owen. He and Nick again started to walk away.

Tiny strode after them. "Wait a fuckin' minute, asshole. You threw a fuckin' beer at me. You think I'm gonna let you walk away from that?"

Owen and Nick stopped again, turning to find Tiny about ten feet away. Vukie was lagging behind, seemingly reluctant to get embroiled in this. Tiny was smiling, but he had a wild look in his eyes. This time it was Nick who spoke up. "Look, man, we didn't throw a beer bottle at you. We've never even seen you before. We're not looking for trouble. Let's just let it go, and we'll get out of here."

"Not you, asswipe. It was this prick." Tiny pointed at Owen.

"It wasn't me," Owen said, anxiety creeping into his voice. "You've got me mixed up with someone else."

"Fuck this talk, man!" Tiny yelled, starting toward Owen. "It's time for you to get your ass kicked!"

Nick, much closer in size to the enormous Tiny than was Owen, stepped in front of Owen. "You're gonna have to kick my ass first."

"Not a problem, dickhead," yelled Tiny as he took a swing at Nick. After hesitating for a moment, Vukie charged Owen.

The Aftermath

Chapter 12

Dante and Ryan emerged from the walkway onto the beach just as Vukie was running into the woods at the opposite end of the beach. Their banter stopped abruptly when they saw the scene awaiting them: Owen doubled over in the sand, his face battered and swollen; a huge man in biker's clothes lying perfectly still, blood oozing from his neck; and Nick, standing motionless with a stunned look on his face, holding a chain.

"What the fuck happened?" shouted Ryan as he ran toward Nick. Dante went over to check on Owen.

Clearly dazed, Nick mumbled something about a fight. Ryan fell to his knees and peered at Tiny, who didn't appear to be breathing. Nudging him twice produced no reaction. Ryan then placed an ear to Tiny's massive chest, listening for a heartbeat. Nothing. He yelled over to Dante, "Holy shit, man, this guy's dead!"

Dante, meanwhile, was tending to Owen, who was semiconscious. After trying unsuccessfully to help him stand up, Dante eased him painfully into a sitting position and knelt down in front of him. Owen nodded when Dante asked if he could hear him but did not respond to any of Dante's other questions.

Reacting to Ryan, Dante walked over to where he and Nick were standing. After briefly surveying Tiny's body, Ryan looked at Nick.

"You OK, man?"

"Yeah, *I'm* OK. But this guy...Man, I didn't mean to do that."

Nick had by now dropped the chain, and Dante noticed it in the sand. "You hit him with that?"

Nick nodded. Dante picked up the chain and put it in his pocket. Turning to Ryan, he said, "Let's get these guys out of here. Then we can figure out what the hell we do next."

Dante and Ryan together helped Owen to his feet. Dante, who was bigger and stronger than Ryan, draped Owen's left arm around his neck and wrapped his right arm around Owen's back, with his hand under Owen's right armpit for support. With Dante half leading and half carrying Owen, the four of them headed up the walkway away from the lake. On the way, Nick filled them in on what had happened at the beach.

When they reached Lakeview Drive, Ryan said, "Let's stop here, figure out our plan. No point in these two guys going back to the party like this until we know what we're doing."

The three of them instinctively looked to Owen, who was the best of all of them—the best they knew—at figuring out how to deal with tough situations. But Owen was still groggy, his breathing labored as a result of his cracked rib and his limited attempts to speak barely coherent. The other boys were on their own.

Dante spoke up first. "We gotta get Owen to a hospital. I don't know what's wrong with him, but he doesn't look right."

"Let's just call the cops," said Nick. "They can bring an ambulance. And we gotta tell the cops what happened." He paused. "I killed that guy," he added, choking up on the last words.

"Take it easy, man," Ryan said. "I don't know about calling the cops. It was just an accident, man."

"I know!" exclaimed Nick. "That's why we gotta call the cops, so I can explain all that."

"Alright, here's what we do," interjected Dante. "First thing we gotta do is get Owen to a hospital; then we'll figure out what we do with the cops." He looked at Nick and Owen. "Me and Ryan're gonna walk up to Kirby's house and find someone that'll drive Owen to the hospital. Sully, you wait here with Owen. We'll be back in like ten minutes."

"Sounds like a plan, man," said Ryan. "You guys just sit tight. This is gonna work out."

Walking up the road toward the Nolans' house, Ryan whispered to Dante, "Sully's fucked, man. He's supposed to fly out to rookie camp tomorrow. No way the cops'll let him leave town now."

"Forget about rookie camp, Ryan. He could end up in jail and not play pro hockey at all."

"Shit. Maybe we shouldn't call the cops. No one'll know who did it."

"What about the guy who kicked the shit outa Owen?" Dante replied. "He was there, he saw what happened."

"But he doesn't know who Sully is. If we get the hell outa here, he'll never see Sully to ID him."

Dante thought for a minute. "No, that won't work. We're talking about a murder here. The cops'll check on all the houses in the area, find out who was around here tonight. They'll catch up with Sully eventually."

"So what the fuck do we do?"

"I don't know, man. Lemme think."

They finished the short walk to the Nolans' house in silence. Dante stopped in front of the house and turned to Ryan. "Here's what we do. We find someone to take Owen to the hospital. But not up here—the one in Pennington."

"I can get Heather to do that," said Ryan.

"OK. Then you take my car and drive Nick home. I'm gonna stay here and call the cops. I'm gonna tell 'em I went down to go swimming and I saw two biker dudes fighting each other on the beach. And that one of 'em swung something and knocked down the other guy, then took off running."

"Why you gonna make up that story?"

"'Cause if the biker we saw running away tells the cops that a high-school kid killed his buddy, maybe the cops'll think he's just saying that to cover for one of the bikers. Especially if I tell my story to the cops first."

Ryan grinned. "That's not bad, man. Not bad at all."

But Dante had a very different plan in mind.

* * *

Dante and Ryan drove the short distance down Lakeview Drive to the walkway, where Nick and Owen were waiting. Heather followed them in her car. After the boys helped Owen into Heather's car, she headed off for the Pennington hospital.

Dante and Ryan then explained their plan to Nick. To their surprise, he balked at it. "No way, man. I gotta tell the cops what happened. I can't run from this."

"Use your head, Sully," Ryan countered. "You wanna piss away your hockey career over some asshole biker who got what was coming to him? Remember, he attacked you guys."

"Yeah, I know. If I explain the whole thing—how they started it, we were just defending ourselves—maybe they won't charge me with anything."

"Sully, the guy's dead," said Dante. "No way you're walking away from this. And you think the Red Wings're gonna like hearing about this? They'll probably cut your ass as soon as they hear. It's not like you can play for them from jail anyway."

Nick continued to protest, insisting that he wanted to turn himself in. After a few minutes of back and forth, Dante said, "Fine, Sully. I guess it is your call." He turned to Ryan. "Remember that police station we passed in the center of town? Why don't you drive Sully there."

"What're you gonna do?" asked Ryan, confused at the change in plans.

"I'm going back up to Kirby's house. The cops'll come out here, and they might come by the house. So we gotta let Kirby know what's going on, get things cleaned up some." Dante turned to Nick and gave him a quick hug. "Good luck, man."

With the car parked on the right edge of the road, the three of them had been standing on the passenger side of the Honda, between the car and the woods. Nick got into the front passenger seat, and Ryan walked around behind the car to get into the driver's seat. As he did, Dante grabbed him. "Fuck all that. Just take him home."

"You serious?"

"Hell yeah, man. We're sticking with our plan. He'll yell and scream at you, but don't pay any attention to that. Just take him home."

As soon as Ryan and Nick drove away, Dante took out his cell phone and called the Kingsbridge Park police. After being connected with an officer on duty, he said, "Hi, my name's Dante Lombardo. I want to report that a guy got killed in a fight at the beach off Lakeview Drive."

"Did you witness the fight, sir?"

"Yeah. I'm the one who killed him."

Chapter 13

It took Vukie about fifteen minutes to make his way through the woods back to the Satan's Knights' cottage. Disoriented from a full day of drinking and drugs, he briefly found himself lost in the woods before finally emerging into the side of the yard farthest away from the beach. He entered the kitchen to find only three guys left in the house. The others had gone into Leeds Beach to hit the bars.

Vukie told them about the fight and about Tiny. He wasn't going to admit to running away or not checking on Tiny, so he lied about how things ended. According to the story Vukie spun, he chased both kids off and then went over to find Tiny dead.

"He wasn't breathing?"

"Not at all, man."

"You check his pulse?"

"Of course I fuckin' checked his pulse. Nothing, man." Having backed himself into a corner with his fabricated ending, Vukie was now fervently hoping Tiny was in fact dead.

"We gotta find those fuckin' kids, man!" one of the bikers shouted.

"Hold up, dude. We don't even know where to look for them," a biker named Bruno said. "We got other shit to worry about first."

"Like what?"

"Lots of people go to that beach. Somebody's gonna find Tiny's body real soon and call the heat. They might've already."

"So what?"

"There'll be cops swarming all over here. We'll all end up in the joint if we don't clean this place up."

"Should we take off?"

"Let's just get the shit outa here. Then we'll go down to the beach and see what's goin' on. If the cops aren't there yet, we might as well call 'em. I don't wanna just leave Tiny's body lying there."

One of the bikers picked up the mirror with meth residue on it while another grabbed a bag of pot from the counter. A third biker was starting to gather up the Wild Turkey and Old Grand Dad bottles when Bruno grabbed him by the shoulder, spinning him around.

"You fuckin' idiot, whiskey's not illegal!" Bruno hissed. "Just grab the weed and the meth."

It took them about fifteen minutes to satisfy themselves that they had collected all the drugs in the house. They put them into a backpack and buried them underneath some leaves and branches a few feet into the surrounding woods. The four of them then headed down to the beach.

* * *

Dante was waiting on Lakeview Drive, at the end of the walkway, when a Kingsbridge Park cruiser with two officers pulled up. After asking Dante for his ID, the older officer—Officer Kapinski—asked Dante to show them to the body.

As they headed down the walkway, Officer Kapinski asked Dante, "So, you want to tell us what happened?"

"Yes, sir." Dante had been rehearsing the story in his head and was eager to tell it to the cops—he wanted to get it out before he forgot any of the details or lost his nerve.

The younger officer recited the Miranda warning to Dante and took out a pen and small pad to take notes on. Dante then told his story. His version of events tracked, as closely as his memory would allow, what Nick had told him—except Dante substituted himself for Nick. He described being accosted by the two bikers, the bikers starting the fight, wresting the chain away from the bigger biker and then swinging it at him, aiming for the guy's midsection but accidentally hitting his throat.

Dante wasn't quite through with his description of the fight when the trio reached the beach. There was a break in Dante's narration while Kapinski checked Tiny's body for a pulse and then called for an ambulance. Turning back to Dante, the officer asked him to continue with his recounting of events. Dante finished his story, and then reached into his pocket and handed Kapinski the chain from the fight. He had carefully wiped it with a rag he'd taken from his car, so the only fingerprints on it were his own. Dante was answering a few questions when

Vukie and the other three Satan's Knights emerged from the walkway onto the beach.

"Is that the motherfucker who killed Tiny?" one of them yelled as they strode toward Dante and the cops. Officer Kapinski stepped forward and led the four men a short distance away from Dante. He talked with them for a few minutes and then led Vukie back to where Dante and the other officer were standing.

Kapinski first asked Vukie if he recognized the person lying in the sand. "Yeah, man, that's Tiny."

"What's his real name?"

"Luther Schmidt. I'm pretty sure. We just call him Tiny, man"

Kapinski then gestured toward Dante and asked Vukie, "Is this the person you saw hit your friend with the chain?"

Dante and Nick were both big kids, about the same height and build, with short-cropped brown hair. Like most kids at the party that night, they both wore shorts and T-shirts. Vukie had been focused on his fight with Owen and had never gotten too close to Nick. He was also drunk, high, and looking to blame someone for Tiny's death. That confluence of factors led to Vukie saying, "Yeah, that's the fuckin' asshole who killed Tiny" and believing every word of it.

After taking down some contact information from the four Satan's Knights, Officer Kapinski sent them on their way. He then continued with his interrogation of

Dante, asking him for the name of his friend who was in the fight with the other biker.

Dante hesitated. Should he give them Owen's name? He wasn't sure Owen would go along with his story. But he hadn't told Ryan about his plan, either, so he couldn't be certain Ryan would back him up on this. He was still thinking about that when Kapinski pressed him.

"I know you probably don't want to get your friend involved in this. But if things happened the way you said they did, he's got nothing to worry about—he didn't do anything wrong. But he's a witness to what happened here tonight, so we're going to need to talk with him." Dante thought about it for another moment and then gave them Owen's name.

After asking a few more questions, Officer Kapinski placed Dante under arrest.

* * *

Ryan dropped Nick off at home at about eleven o'clock that night. Nick spoke only briefly to his parents before going to his room and closing the door. Besides being sore as hell from the fight, his head was swirling with conflicting emotions. He was pissed off at Ryan and Dante, concerned about Owen, relieved that he wasn't under arrest, fearful that the incident wasn't really behind him, and curious about how the cops reacted to Dante's story about the bikers. After repeatedly calling both Dante and Owen but reaching only their voice mails, he tried unsuccessfully to go to sleep. It was just before 1:00 a.m. when his cell phone rang. It was Owen.

"Where are you, man?" Nick asked anxiously. "You alright?"

"Yeah, I'm fine. A few cuts and bruises, and they think one of my ribs is broken. Maybe a concussion. But I'm feeling better; I'm not groggy like I was."

"Are you still in the hospital?"

"No, no, I'm home. They checked me and then let me go." Owen paused, fearful of the answer to his next question. His memory of what had happened after the fight was hazy, but he had a clear memory of the fight itself. "So that biker you were fighting…?"

Nick said in a quiet voice, "He's dead."

"What happened afterward? I don't remember much between the fight and the hospital."

Nick explained how he had wanted to turn himself into the police but Ryan, over Nick's protests, had driven him home instead. Ryan told Nick on the ride home that Dante was staying behind to feed a story to the cops about how he saw two bikers fighting, with one hitting the other with a chain.

"So where's Dante now?" Owen asked.

"I don't know. I've called him a bunch of time, left messages. I haven't heard a word from him."

"Did you try Ryan to see if he heard from him?"

"No, never even thought of that," Nick said. "I'm not sure I'm really thinking straight, to tell you the truth."

"Just sit tight. I'm going try Dante and Ryan. I'll call you back in a couple of minutes."

Owen called back five minutes later. "I can't get a hold of either of them."

"Jeez, man. I'm supposed to go to the airport tomorrow around noon. I gotta know what's going on."

"Listen, just plan to be on that flight. We'll track those guys down in the morning and find out what happened. But it probably went just like Dante said—he told that story to the cops, and they bought it."

"I don't know, man. This is crazy."

"Get some sleep. We'll talk in the morning."

* * *

Owen got up at eight o'clock and began calling Dante and Ryan. Nick started doing the same thing at about eight fifteen. Neither answered; Ryan was still sleeping, and Dante's phone sat with his wallet and watch in the safe of the Kingsbridge Park police station.

A pissed-off Anthony Lombardo put up bail for his son shortly after nine thirty that morning, and Dante was released into his custody. The first fifteen minutes of the car ride home consisted of Dante explaining to his father what had happened—he told him the same story he'd told the police—interrupted by profanity-laced tirades from his father. Dante ignored several calls from Owen and Nick during this time.

After Dante finished his account of the previous night's events and his father (temporarily) stopped berating him, Dante asked his father to stop at a gas station so he could use the restroom. From there Dante called Owen and then Nick and told them the same story: he told the cops he saw two bikers fighting; the cops seemed to buy it; and he didn't know what the cops did after that, but it looked like things were going to work out fine.

As soon as Nick hung up with Dante, he called Owen. Nick told Owen that he was still thinking about turning himself in. Owen felt for his friend and considered that for a moment. "Look, you should get on that plane to Detroit. We don't know how this is all gonna shake out, but right now it looks like you're gonna be alright."

"You're probably right. But this is gonna weigh on me, man."

"Don't let it. You didn't do anything wrong. The biker started the fight, and what you did was an accident. You were trying to defend yourself, not kill the guy."

"I know," said Nick. "But still, what if the cops talk to the bikers and believe their story?"

"Just go to rookie camp and try to put this outa your head. You can always come back later and tell the cops what happened. But just let things play out here for a while before you decide to do something like that."

"Alright, man."

"Hey, how are you feeling?" asked Owen.

"I'm OK. My jaw is a little sore and I got a cut over my eye, but nothing serious. I'll be fine. What about you?"

"My rib hurts, but that's about it. My head feels fine."

That's good, man, glad to hear it."

"Hey, listen, good luck, bro. Call me tomorrow or the next day when you get a chance."

Chapter 14

On Monday afternoon Owen was lying on the couch in his basement with the Red Sox game on TV. The game was not garnering much of his attention, though. He was brooding over the events of the previous night when his thoughts were interrupted by the buzzing of his cell phone. When he saw Dante's name on the caller-ID screen, he hurriedly answered it.

"Hey, what's up, Dante?"

"Nothing, man. Hey, did Sully get on his flight?"

"Yeah, he's gone."

"Good. You home?"

"Yeah, why?"

"Now that Sully's left, I gotta talk to you about something. I'm comin' over."

Dante arrived five minutes later. A couple of Owen's siblings were home, so he and Dante retreated to his bedroom for privacy. Dante proceeded to tell Owen the real story of what had transpired up in Kingsbridge Park after Ryan drove away with Nick. Owen's initial shock was soon replaced with concern for Dante.

"You can't do that, Dante. You can't go to jail for something you didn't do."

"It's done, Owen. I can't go back up there and say, 'Oh, by the way, everything I told you last night? I just made that up.' Besides, that would put Sully's head on the chopping block."

"Shit, man," said an increasingly frustrated Owen. "This is a mess."

Dante managed a smile. "You think you're pissed now, wait till you hear this." He paused. "I told the cops you were the other kid in the fight, that you could back up my story."

Owen hurled the Nerf basketball he'd been holding across the room. "Goddamn it, Dante! You want me to lie under oath for you?"

"Not for me, Owen," Dante said quietly. "For Sully."

Owen exhaled loudly. After a moment he said, "I guess this is between you and Nick. If he goes along with it, I will too."

"Sorry for putting you in a tough spot, man. I just figured I could count on you more than Ryan, ya know?"

"When you gonna tell Sully about this?"

"Tomorrow or the next day. I wanna let him get settled out in Detroit before I spring this on him."

"Sooner rather than later's probably better. You know he's worried about this."

"I know, I'm sure he is. But I wanna go through with this—I don't want him coming back to take the fall. I'm just thinking that the longer he's out there, the harder it'll be for him to walk away from camp."

* * *

Rookie camp was going well for Nick. Despite his initial nervousness, he quickly learned that he could skate, shoot, and hit better than almost every other prospect in camp. The feedback from the coaches was also positive and encouraging. He was beginning to think he had a real shot at making the Red Wings that year.

The on-ice sessions, off-ice training, and team meetings kept Nick preoccupied with hockey during almost every waking minute. The fight at Lake Winnipesaukee did weigh on his mind, though, especially during the relatively rare moments of downtime or when lying in bed at night. He called Dante on Tuesday night and again Wednesday morning, but Dante let both calls go to voice mail.

Dante finally placed a call to Nick late Wednesday morning. He was hoping Nick was tied up and that he'd get his voice mail—he wanted to be able to explain to Nick what he'd done without interruptions or questions. The timing of his call was impeccable, as Nick was in the middle of an intrasquad scrimmage. Dante left a lengthy message and then turned off his phone for a few hours.

It was lunchtime before Nick had a chance to check his phone for texts or voice mails. Stunned by the message he heard, he took a few minutes to gather himself before calling Dante back. After several failed attempts to reach Dante, Nick went into a 2:00 p.m. team meeting. He emerged from the meeting at three fifteen, recalling virtually nothing of what had been said at it, and immediately tried Dante again. This time he got through.

"What the hell, man, what were you thinking? You can't do that!" he exclaimed as soon as Dante answered.

"Sully, I've thought a lot about this. This is what I want to do. I'd rather do a little time than see you blow an NHL career."

"Look, Dante, it's not like I don't appreciate what you're doing. It's unbelievable that you would do that for me. But I can't let you take the blame for this. I'm coming back, man. I'm gonna tell the police what really happened."

"Forget about it, Sully. It's over. The cops've talked to me like four times. I've given them a sworn statement. I'm gonna plead guilty to some lesser charge that my lawyer can negotiate."

"You got a lawyer?"

"Yeah, some guy that Owen's dad lined me up with."

"What's Owen think about this?"

"At first he didn't like it, but now I think he gets that it's the best thing for everyone."

Nick thought for a moment. "Fuck all that, I'm coming back."

"Nick, think about it for a minute. It's too late. I already confessed. Even if you tell the cops you did it, I'm sticking to my story. And they're gonna believe me. That asshole biker that beat up Owen told the cops that I'm the one who did it. I gave the chain to the cops, and it's got my fingerprints on it, not yours. This is all wrapped up, Sully."

Nick spent a few more minutes trying to talk Dante out of it before realizing it was futile. "Shit, Dante, I don't know what else to say."

"Look, man, this is for the best. If they got you for this, your hockey career is dead before it even starts. Me, it's not like I was going to Harvard. I was gonna join the goddamn army. My lawyer says I shouldn't have to do more than a year, maybe eighteen months. When I get out, I can probably still join the army. That's what I wanna do. I'll be fine, man."

Another minute or two of awkward conversation followed before Nick thanked Dante once again and then hung up. It would be ten years before they spoke again.

* * *

Over the course of the next three weeks, the Kingsbridge Park police department's investigation of Luther Schmidt's death—including affidavits from Dante, Owen, and Vukie—and the plea bargain negotiations between Dante's lawyer and the DA's office proceeded on parallel tracks. The DA had initially threatened to charge Dante with voluntary manslaughter—killing someone intentionally but doing so in the heat of passion rather than with prior intent. That charge, in New Hampshire, carried a prison sentence of up to thirty years. After about ten days of back and forth, Dante's lawyer had convinced the DA to accept a guilty plea to involuntary manslaughter, which was essentially killing someone recklessly but unintentionally. The haggling over how much jail time Dante would have to do continued for another week. The state sentencing guidelines for involuntary manslaughter were twenty-four to sixty months. Based on consistent testimony that Schmidt had started the fight, Dante's clean record, and his cooperation in the case, the DA's office agreed to accept a guilty plea in exchange for a recommendation of a thirty-month sentence, with parole eligibility after fourteen months. The plea bargain received court approval in early August. On August 11, Dante reported to the New Hampshire State Prison in Concord to begin his sentence.

Ten Years Later

Chapter 15

The elegant facade of the St. Regis Hotel towers twenty stories over the bustle of Fifth Avenue in New York. Located in midtown Manhattan, just four blocks south of Central Park, the five-star hotel has been graced with the presence of heads of state, A-list movie stars, and the Rolling Stones. On this cold Tuesday evening in January, the St. Regis was hosting the Detroit Red Wings.

A consistent NHL powerhouse, the Red Wings were in town to play the New York Rangers the following night. Detroit was ensconced in second place in the NHL's sixteen-team Eastern Conference and poised to make another strong challenge for the Stanley Cup. Their high-powered offense was led by Henrik Lindberg, a fifteen-year veteran and team captain. Anchoring the team's sturdy defense was assistant captain and perennial all-star Nick Sullivan.

Though just twenty-eight, Nick was already a ten-year veteran and one of the team's stars. He had surprised many Red Wings fans and media members by making the team as an eighteen-year-old straight out of high school. After a somewhat uneven rookie year, Nick blossomed into one of the team's top four defensemen in his second season. His first selection to the NHL all-star game came at the tender age of twenty-two, and hockey pundits now regarded him as one of the league's top defensemen. He was in the final season of a four-year multimillion-dollar contract and was in a strong position to become one of the NHL's two or three highest-paid defensemen following the current season.

At ten o'clock that night, Nick was lying on his hotel bed, watching a movie on HBO, when he was surprised to hear the phone in his room ring. Everyone he would expect to hear from—a coach, teammates, his parents—would call his cell phone. And he didn't think anyone beyond that group would know what hotel he was staying at, much less what room he was in. After hesitating a moment, he picked up the phone. "Hello?"

"Sully?"

"Who's this?"

There was a mirthless chuckle. "You don't recognize my voice?" Hearing no response from Nick, he continued. "It's Ryan Cunningham."

"Holy shit! Ryan Cunningham? Really?"

"Yeah, man, it's really me. And just so you don't think this is some asshole pulling a prank on you, I can tell you all about the time you kicked me out of my mom's basement so you and Mary Beth what's-her-name could have some quality time to yourselves."

"I can't believe it, man." Nick was as confused as he was surprised. He had not had any contact with Cunningham in years. "What've you been up to?"

"You know me, man. Nothing good. Hey, listen, though—I gotta talk to you."

"Sure. What's up?"

"No, man, gotta be in person."

"Everything OK?" asked Nick.

"More or less. Can we meet somewhere tomorrow? I know you got a game at night, but during the day sometime?"

"What's this all about, Ryan?"

"I'll tell you when I see you. How 'bout we meet for lunch somewhere?"

"Wait, are you in *New York*?"

"Yeah, I'm down here for a few days. So, there must be a restaurant in your hotel, right? Can you meet me there at noon tomorrow?"

Nick paused, thinking. "We got a morning skate at ten thirty. I doubt I'll be back by noon. How 'bout one?"

"You got it. See you then, man." Cunningham hung up before Nick could ask any more questions.

Nick watched the end of the movie and then went to bed. Though sleep usually came easily to him, he lay awake for a long time that night, trying to shake an uneasy feeling.

* * *

Of his three closest friends from high school, Nick had kept in touch only with Owen. Owen had attended Bates College in Maine and then spent a year as an intern at a venture-capital firm outside of Boston. He had been toying with the idea of following in his father's footsteps to law school, but, entranced by his taste of venture-capital deal making, he elected to attend business school instead. After graduating from the prestigious Tuck School of Business, Owen took a job with Hart & Gates, a Boston consulting firm that specialized in advising growing technology companies—which abounded in the greater Boston area—on capital raising and strategic partnering opportunities. He was currently a third-year associate at that firm, working ungodly hours but making very good money, learning how to structure and negotiate deals and building a reputation as a savvy advisor. Nick saw Owen frequently in the off-season, either hosting him at Nick's lakeside townhouse in Grosse Point, just outside of Detroit, or visiting him at his Beacon Hill condo when Nick returned to New Hampshire to see his parents.

    The arc of Dante's life over the last ten years had veered in a direction completely opposite that of Owen's. After his plea bargain for the Kingsbridge Park incident, he served fourteen months in prison and remained on parole for one year after his release. He tried joining in the army as soon as he got out of jail but learned that he could not enlist until his parole was complete. Biding his time until eligible for the army, Dante spent that year living in a studio apartment in a tough section of Manchester and working a series of tedious, low-paying jobs.

    Nick and Owen tried contacting Dante numerous times, both during and after his jail stint, with no success. They visited the state prison on more than one occasion, but Dante declined to see them. Through the lawyer Dante had used in negotiating his plea bargain, Owen was able to learn when Dante was released. But several calls and visits to his father's house were fruitless—Dante was never there, at least according to his father, who, on Dante's instructions, refused to divulge Dante's new cellphone number or where he was living.

Shortly before Christmas of that year, Owen heard from a friend that Dante was working at the Home Depot in Manchester. When Nick was in Boston to play the Bruins around that time, he and Owen drove up to New Hampshire and visited the Home Depot together, but Dante was not working then. Owen tried again about a week later and found Dante there, but Dante refused to speak with him.

Dante found it curious that he never heard of any attempts by Cunningham to get in touch with him. He chalked that up to Cunningham being pissed at him for lying about what he was going to tell the cops that night in Kingsbridge Park, but he sometimes wondered if there wasn't more than that at play.

Just as Nick and Owen were baffled by why Dante would cut off all contact with them, Dante himself found it hard to put his finger on exactly why he was doing that. Some days he was resentful that they let him take the fall for what Nick did (apparently forgetting their attempts to talk him out of that and the fact that his clever actions would have almost certainly thwarted any effort by them to undermine his confession). Other times he felt embarrassed by the fact that he was now a felon, working dead-end jobs—a felony conviction scared away a lot of potential employers—and living in squalor, while Nick and Owen were clearly on track for bigger and better things.

He also realized he would be joining the army before long, putting Pennington and Kingsbridge Park in his rearview mirror—for good, he hoped—and thought he might as well cut ties now rather than simply postpone the inevitable. The day his parole ended, Dante enlisted in the army. He left town after saying good-bye to no one but his father.

The only thing Nick heard about Dante during his four-year stint in the army were rumors that he had seen heavy-duty action in Afghanistan. The next news to reach him, roughly three years ago, was that after leaving the army, Dante had settled in Rhode Island and gotten married. Owen obtained a phone number for Dante, and he and Nick left several messages with his wife, which were never returned. Frustrated, Nick waited over a year before his next call to Dante, when he once again reached his wife. On that call, Nick learned that Dante had left his wife almost a year earlier. She believed he had headed to Arizona or New Mexico, but she had not heard from him since he'd left, and she had no way of getting in contact with him. She also told Nick that just weeks after Dante had left, she had learned she was pregnant. Their daughter was now four months old, she told him at the time; Dante did not know she existed. From time to time, Nick sent money to Dante's wife, but he had heard nothing more about Dante since that conversation with her over a year ago.

From what little Nick knew about Cunningham, he had fared little better than Dante over the ten years since they had graduated from St. Xavier. Owen and, to a lesser extent, Nick had stayed in touch with Cunningham for about two years after graduation. However, it soon became apparent to all three of them that Cunningham's path in life was significantly diverging from Owen's and Nick's, and Cunningham gradually lost contact with them. Nick knew that Cunningham had dropped out of community college after less than a year and then spent a few years banging around Pennington before moving to Manchester. The next thing Nick heard about Cunningham, through Owen, was that he had lost a job he had with a construction company and was collecting unemployment. There were also rumors that Cunningham was gambling a lot, but the details had been sketchy. Nick had heard nothing else about him in the last few years—until his call that evening.

Chapter 16

Thanks to Manhattan traffic, the one-and-a-half-mile cab ride from Madison Square Garden, where the Red Wings held their morning skate, back to the St. Regis took over half an hour. So it was shortly after one o'clock on Wednesday afternoon when Nick walked into the hotel lobby and headed for the tavern. Cunningham was waiting for him at the tavern's entrance. Clad in work boots, blue jeans, a tattered leather jacket, and a baseball cap and sporting a bandage wrapped around his right hand, Cunningham stood in stark contrast to the well-heeled clientele streaming in and out of the restaurant.

Nick strode up to Ryan and extended his hand. "Good to see ya, man."

"You too, Sully." They shared a quick hug, and then Cunningham said, "Let's take a walk."

"I thought we were having lunch here."

"We need a little more privacy."

Cunningham walked through the lobby, with Nick a half step behind. When they reached the sidewalk, Cunningham turned up the collar of his worn leather jacket and turned left toward Fifth Avenue. Nick was always amazed by how loud the streets of New York were. They walked in silence for a minute, with Nick waiting for Cunningham to explain why he wanted to meet and Cunningham rehashing in his head the script for what was sure to be a difficult conversation. Nick decided to break the ice.

"Hey, I gotta ask you something. How'd you reach me in my room last night?"

"Whaddaya mean?"

"How'd you know what hotel to call? And you must've known my room number too, 'cause they won't put the call through if you just ask for me by name."

"A guy I know told me that the Red Wings always stay at the St. Regis. So I went over there last night and gave the girl at the desk a few bucks to put my call through to your room."

Nick laughed. "Well, here's my cell number if you need to reach me again." He handed him a slip of paper. Ryan put it in his pocket but continued walking in silence.

"So what's up, man? You OK?" Nick asked. "You're acting awful mysterious."

"Here's the thing, man. I need to ask you to do something for me."

Still walking down Fifth Avenue, Nick turned to look at Cunningham for a moment, waiting for him to go on.

Cunningham continued to dance around the subject. "I'm in trouble, and you're the only guy who can help me out of it."

Nick glanced at his bandaged hand. "What kind of trouble?"

"I owe a lot of money. And I owe it to some guys that you don't want to owe money to."

"You mean, like, the Mafia?"

"I don't know if these guys are in the Mafia. But they're definitely mob guys. You know, like, professional crooks."

"Is this gambling debts?"

"Pretty much, yeah."

"How much you owe?"

"To be honest with ya, I don't even know. The way they do the fuckin' interest, I can't even keep track of it. But it's a lot."

"Like, a few grand?"

"More than that."

"Ten grand?"

"Keep going."

"Holy shit, Ryan."

"I know, man. It was originally around twenty-two grand in gambling losses. But with the vig on that, I think it's close to thirty. And then I fucked up some other thing I was doing to try to pay it off. So now I'm into these bastards for, like, more than fifty grand. And these motherfuckers gave me a choice. I gotta get you to help me out, or they're gonna fuckin' kill me."

"You want me to give you fifty thousand dollars?" Nick asked incredulously.

Cunningham paused. "No, Sully. I want you to throw your game against the Bruins in a couple of weeks."

* * *

Gambling on hockey is not as popular as gambling on football or even basketball. But Las Vegas posts betting odds on all kinds of sports, so there is still plenty of money wagered on NHL games. Wagering on football and basketball games is based primarily on the point spread. Betting works differently for hockey games and is generally done using a money line. To win a bet on a hockey game, your team doesn't need to win by a certain number of goals (or lose by less than a certain number of goals); it simply needs to win the game. The money line determines how much you are paid for picking the winner, with underdogs paying more than favorites. For example, the money line for an NHL game might be Philadelphia +120, Pittsburgh -140. That means Pittsburgh is the favorite, and you have to bet $140 on Pittsburgh to win $100. On the other hand, a $100 bet on the underdog Philadelphia Flyers would pay $120.

Gamblers or mob guys have occasionally succeeded in paying players to negatively influence the outcome of a game so that gamblers can win by betting on the opposing team. The most common scheme is point shaving, which occurs when a player on the favored team intentionally screws up so his team wins by less than the point spread. An even more repugnant variant of that is throwing a game—a player ensuring that his team loses the game. For gamblers betting on hockey games using the money line, rigging the game through point shaving is not an option (as there is no point spread involved);

getting a player to throw the game is the only means of ensuring that they win their bet.

Not every player is in a position to ensure that his team loses—or wins by less than the point spread. A defensive lineman in football can avoid making any tackles in a game, but he has ten teammates on the field to make the play; and he can have no impact on how much his team scores. A quarterback, on the other hand, can pretty much ensure a putrid offensive output by his team, and a well-placed interception or fumble can even put points on the board for the opposition. Point-shaving scandals in basketball have typically involved more than one player on a team because of the limited impact a single poor performance can have on the game. In hockey, having a forward in the tank can do little good. The player in the best position to ensure a loss is the goalie. But a defenseman is not a bad option. A series of poor plays or missed assignments can almost guarantee a couple of extra goals for the opposing team. And because most NHL games are decided by two goals or less, that can be enough to swing the outcome of the game.

* * *

Nick stopped dead on the crowded Fifth Avenue sidewalk, drawing a swear from the young woman who bumped into him from behind. His first thought was to punch Cunningham. "Are you crazy? You're an asshole for even bringing that up."

"Take it easy, man. I wouldn't ask you if my ass wasn't on the line. They're gonna fuckin' kill me, Sully."

Nick started walking again and thought for a moment. "Can you go to the police?"

"Yeah, right. What are they gonna do, arrest these guys 'cause I said they threatened me? Besides, they'd probably kill me anyway."

"Who are these guys?"

"What difference does it make? You don't know them."

"Look, maybe I could lend you some money to help you pay these guys off."

"You don't get it, man. I'm past the point where I can just pay these guys off. This one guy's got it in his head that he can make a big score on this Bruins game if you help us out."

"Forget it, Ryan. There's not a chance in hell I'm doing that. Don't even bring it up again."

"You know, I didn't want to have to do this, but I got no choice. If you don't help me out here, Sully, I'm gonna go to the cops and tell 'em what really happened at the beach in Kingsbridge Park that night."

Nick was silent for a minute and then said, "It's too late, Ryan. That was ten years ago. Dante's already done time for that. That's over."

"I did some looking into this, Nick, because, you know, I'm kinda desperate here. There's no statute of limitations for murder, so they could still charge you for that. And that double jeopardy shit doesn't count here.

They can't try you twice for the same thing, but they can try two different people for the same thing."

Nick was getting angry. "It won't work, asshole. They've got Dante's confession. They're not gonna just ignore that."

"Dante's disappeared, man. No one knows where he is. If I tell the cops what I saw on the beach that night, I bet they buy it. Especially without Dante around to contradict it."

Nick said nothing. Cunningham continued, "Besides, even if for some reason you don't get convicted for this, there's gonna be a ton of publicity. A big NHL star accused of murder. You think the Red Wings are gonna like that? Or how 'bout your mom and dad? You never told them what happened, did ya?"

Nick stopped and shoved Cunningham, knocking him into a street sign. "Get the fuck away from me. And don't ever talk to me again."

Cunningham was smirking now, regaining his composure as Nick lost his. "It's not that simple, Nick. Think about it, man. Fuck up a few times, let a few guys get behind you, make sure the Bruins win. No one will ever know about it, and I'm out of a big jam. Wouldn't that be easier than facing a fuckin' murder charge?"

Cunningham turned and started walking in the opposite direction. Looking back over his shoulder, he called out to Nick, "I'll be in touch."

Chapter 17

It was a cold Monday afternoon in early January—nine days prior to Nick's encounter with Cunningham—and Vinnie Spinelli was holding court at the kitchen table in his townhouse in Revere, a working-class coastal city just north of Boston. The thirty-six-year-old Spinelli stood a shade over six feet, with large hands and a well-muscled body. His ruggedly handsome face was capped with wavy black hair and sported a scar over his left eye and a neatly trimmed Van Dyke. Surrounded by his three lieutenants—he at least referred to them as lieutenants, even though no formal title had been bestowed on Spinelli that would justify such a designation for his underlings—Spinelli was getting his weekly report on how each of his three businesses had fared the previous week and collecting the spoils of those operations. Despite the lack of recognition from the powers that be in organized crime and the youthfulness of its leadership, Spinelli's gang didn't lack for structure. One of his lieutenants, Carmine Benevento, oversaw his bookmaking operation; a second was in charge of prostitution; and a third, Jimmy O'Heir, ran his drug-dealing network. He paid his lieutenants each Monday out of the previous week's take, including enough money for them to pay the guys working under them.

Business, as usual, was good. There seemed to be no shortage of people willing to indulge in the illicit services Spinelli offered. Benevento was particularly exuberant when he turned over the gambling receipts, which were boosted by action on the spate of college bowl games the previous week.

"Here you go, Vinny. Twenty-eight thousand three hundred forty dollars! That's a fuckin' record, man."

"Nice, Carmine, nice! I'll make sure there's a little extra in your envelope today."

"Thanks, boss."

"Now how we doin' wit' collections? You know I don't like carryin' deadbeats who don't pay up."

"Not bad. We got five guys who owe us more than five grand. But four of them paid us something last week. So they're workin' it down."

"These guys know we take this shit seriously?"

"Oh yeah. My guys've roughed 'em up a little."

"Don't go too far. Those cocksuckers won't be paying us jack shit if they're lyin' in a fuckin' hospital bed."

"I know, Vinny. We got it covered."

"What about that scumbag from New Hampshire that's into us for, like, twenty-five Gs or something? You get anything from him?"

"No, we pushed him pretty hard. I just don't think he's got a fuckin' dime to give us. But me and Jimmy got an idea on how he can pay down his debt."

"Let's hear it."

* * *

For many years, beginning in the 1950s, organized crime in New England had been just that—organized, with a clear hierarchy and reporting structure. The Palermo family, based in Providence, Rhode Island, had controlled things throughout the region. They ran organized crime in Rhode Island and had underbosses in Boston, Portland, Maine, and a few other New England cities overseeing criminal activities in those areas.

A cut of the earnings from drug dealing, gambling, prostitution, and loan-sharking always flowed uphill. Small-time bookies, pimps, and the like paid tribute money to the local underboss or, more likely, a capo working for the underboss. They didn't receive much in return for those payments, unless you count not getting beaten or killed. The handful of underbosses scattered around New England paid a share of their earnings to the Palermo family in exchange for keeping a position relatively high up the criminal food chain. The Palermo family, in turn, paid a portion of its earnings to the Salvaggio family, one of the Five Families running organized crime in New York. The Salvaggio family did little for the Palermos, occasionally providing them with some muscle or mediating disputes with other factions of the New England organization. However, the implicit threat the Salvaggio family represented to those who might cross swords with the Palermo family was almost always enough to keep peace and keep the Palermos in charge.

The structure of New England organized crime began to experience serious erosion in the 1990s. Well-financed federal investigations had sent many of the top members of the Palermo family, along with the three Antonino brothers, the Boston-based group running things in Massachusetts and southern New Hampshire, to prison. Also contributing to attrition in the leadership ranks was death, both natural (a few of the family heads had reached their eighties and nineties) and unnatural (as ambitious young mobsters battled each other to ascend within the organization).

By the end of the first decade of the new century, the structure of New England crime was in shambles. All top members of the Palermo family were either dead or doing long stints in federal prison, and there were gaps in the leadership structure even below that. Various individuals stepped in to fill vacancies—sometimes with the imprimatur of the Salvaggio family, sometimes not. In general, though, the "new blood" was less respected, and in many cases less suited for the job, than their predecessors. As a result, the hierarchy of New England organized crime was, depending on one's perspective, either fluid and rife with opportunity, or chaotic and beset with violence.

It was into this landscape that Vincent Spinelli strode, feet stomping and elbows flailing. Raised in Chelsea, a hardscrabble city just north of Boston, he and a few friends got their start in the business by knocking off liquor stores and convenience marts as teenagers. Spinelli was smart, tough, and a little crazy, all of which served him well as he gradually climbed the criminal ladder. By the time he was in his early twenties, he ran a crew of eight guys who specialized in robbing drug dealers and pimps—the kinds of victims who don't report the thefts to the police. Those robberies did, however, capture the attention of a capo who controlled—or tried to control—organized crime on Boston's North Shore and was none too pleased to see his dealers and pimps repeatedly coming up short in their tribute payments.

After a bit of digging, the capo discovered who was responsible for the holdups, and one afternoon he and a few of his men paid a visit to Spinelli's apartment. After complimenting Spinelli on the proficiency with which he carried out his jobs, he explained to him exactly how much Spinelli needed to kick up to him for the privilege of being allowed to run roughshod over the North Shore criminal element. Spinelli, of course, didn't like paying a cut of his spoils to someone who contributed and risked nothing. But, at least initially, he recognized it as a cost of doing business.

By the time Spinelli was in his midthirties, he had climbed a few rungs in the mob hierarchy. His crew now numbered about twenty-five. Some of his guys still did robberies, but Spinelli also had guys dealing drugs, running whores, and taking bets for him. His operation spanned most of the northeastern quadrant of the state. Spinelli certainly didn't have a monopoly on criminal activity in that area, but he had a presence in all of the decent-sized cities there. As Spinelli's stature and income increased, so too did his ambition. He was constantly looking for ways to grow his business and expand his territory—even if that meant stepping on other people's toes.

Spinelli was also becoming disenchanted with paying a cut of his earnings to the mobsters in Boston. He thought they lacked smarts and vision and were deserving of neither his money nor his respect. Centered in his crosshairs was the guy to whom he was now paying tribute directly—the current underboss for eastern Massachusetts, Romero Matricula.

* * *

It was nine o'clock on a Thursday night, and the Horseshoe Pub in Revere was hopping. People were two deep the length of the bar, the handful of tall tables in front of the bar were all full, and there was a waiting line to play darts. Unlike some of the newer Revere nightspots closer to the water, this was a working-class crowd, with more patrons north of age forty than south of thirty. There were two TVs over the bar—consoles, not flat-screens—one tuned in to the Bruins game and the other to a Keno channel. A few years ago, the bar would've reeked of cigarette smoke; now it smelled like peanuts and stale beer.

    Cunningham was nervous as he walked into the bar. He didn't like being summoned to a meeting by Carmine Benevento under any circumstances, and he liked it considerably less when he owed him over $25,000. Cunningham had run up his gambling debts through a bookie named TJ Rousseau, who worked for Benevento. He'd first met Benevento about a month ago, when he'd started missing his payments. Benevento and two other men, one of whom was casually brandishing a crowbar, had paid him a visit at home. Benevento emphatically made the point that they didn't like people missing payments. The crowbar-wielding guy, whose name was Ernesto Fernandez, just stared at Cunningham impassively, but the other goon delivered several vicious punches to Cunningham's stomach and kidneys to underscore Benevento's message. That was the only other time Cunningham had seen Benevento before tonight.

    Benevento, O'Heir, and Fernandez were seated at a table near the back of the narrow pub, drinking longneck Buds. Immediately after Cunningham entered, Fernandez waved him over to the table. Benevento pointed silently to the empty chair, and Cunningham took a seat. To ratchet up the tension, Benevento remained silent for what felt to Cunningham like an eternity before speaking.

    "I understand you haven't been making the payments you owe us," he finally said evenly.

"I'm tryin' to pull—"

"Shut the fuck up," Benevento interrupted, quietly but with such intensity that Cunningham stopped in midsyllable and instinctively sat back in his seat.

"We got a new payment plan for you. This is how it's gonna work. Every other Friday, you're gonna make a trip to New York City for us and pick up a package. Then you're gonna make a couple stops on the way home—Lawrence, Haverhill, Lynn—and drop off part of that package. Then you bring the rest of it back to us. It's gonna take you all fuckin' day—you gotta leave here around seven in the morning, and it'll be at least seven at night before you get back here with our stuff. We'll pay you a thousand for each run."

"Am I picking up drugs?"

Benevento sneered, "What the fuck you think you're muling for us, bouquets of roses?"

"It's heroin," said O'Heir. "You got a problem with that?"

"Why you askin' him if he's got a problem, Jimmy?" said Benevento with a cold smile. "He's got no fuckin' choice." He turned to Cunningham. "You start tomorrow."

"I'm supposed to work tomorrow," said Cunningham. He wasn't really challenging Benevento, just whining.

"So get fuckin' sick," Benevento growled malevolently. "Listen, kid, we're not fuckin' around here. You owe us a shitload of money. And you obviously got no way of paying it. So you gotta do this, plain and simple."

"Will I get paid tomorrow?"

Benevento laughed. "What are you, fuckin' retarded? We don't give you the money. It just works down your debt."

Benevento and Fernandez both stood to leave. After dropping forty dollars on the table to cover the bill, Benevento said to Cunningham, "Jimmy here's gonna give you all the details for the pickups and drop-offs. The last guy he had doin' this decided to sample some of the merchandise. You don't wanna know what we did to him." He then leaned in toward Cunningham and draped an arm around his shoulder. "*Don't* fuck this up."

Chapter 18

Sergeant Sara Dunleavy slid into the front passenger seat of the squad car, holding two large coffees. She was an attractive woman in her midtwenties whose standard police uniform was complemented by diamond-stud earrings and stylish sunglasses. She handed one of the coffees to her partner, Herman Knowings, who was sitting behind the wheel and fiddling with the console buttons, trying to coax more out of the car's heater. It was late morning on a raw Friday in January. The temperature was hovering around thirty-two degrees, and it was just beginning to sleet. Dunleavy shivered and brushed some ice off her jacket and hat. Knowings smiled gratefully. "Many thanks. I owe you one."

"You can buy me a hot sub for lunch if we ever finish up here."

"Deal," Knowings said, slurping his coffee.

Dunleavy and Knowings had been paired together for about eighteen months, beginning shortly after Knowings joined the New York City Police Department. Despite having very different backgrounds, they had developed a strong bond during that time. They found that not only did they work well together, but they seemed to have similar values and attitudes about things—they just looked at the world the same way. Neither could remember the last time they'd had a job-related disagreement.

They were parked in an alley in the Fort Greene section of Brooklyn, a block away from a restaurant named Mel's, providing backup on a narcotics operation. Two detectives from the narcotics unit had developed information that the owner of Mel's was a drug dealer operating pretty high up the distribution food chain. According to their information, he was buying heroin directly from a Texas crew that smuggled it over the US border from Mexico and reselling it to numerous dealer networks in New York, New Jersey, and New England. The detectives had managed to plant a bug in the back room of the restaurant and had spent two weeks building a case against him. Today was the day they intended to bust him.

The plan was to listen in until they heard a drug transaction take place. That would give them probable cause to storm the back room, where they expected to find the restaurant owner with a large stash of drugs. If the dealer he sold to was still there, they'd bust him too. If the detectives saw the buyer leave Mel's before they raided it, they'd call Dunleavy and Knowings. The narcotics cops knew there was a decent chance that the buyer would get away, with only one car in position to snare him. But that was a risk they had to live with—the operation wasn't big enough to justify the commitment of more squad cars to it. Besides, the owner of Mel's was the real target here; anyone else they busted was just icing on the cake.

"So these detectives seem pretty excited about this bust, huh?" Knowings commented to his partner.

"Yeah, lately there've been a lot of ODs in the borough from black-tar heroin," Dunleavy replied. "Its purity level is supposed to be over eighty percent. They think this guy may be the source of that heroin."

"I saw a little heroin when I was an MP in Afghanistan. What I saw was white. I've never seen black heroin."

"A lot of the heroin from Mexico is black—kind of a black, gooey substance. I think that's the only place in the world that black tar comes from."

"Why is it black in Mexico and white everywhere else?"

"Some of the Mexican cartels synthesize heroin from poppies using a different process than what's used in Afghanistan and Southeast Asia. It's that and the stuff they cut the heroin with down there—including coffee and brown sugar."

"Is this Mexican black-tar shit more pure?" asked Knowings.

"Not necessarily," replied Dunleavy. "Mexican heroin used to have much lower purity levels than Asian heroin because the chemists there were less experienced in producing heroin. But about fifteen, twenty years ago, the cartels started bringing in expert Asian chemists to synthesize their heroin for them, and the purity levels jumped. A lot of the Mexican smack is still dark, but now its potency can match or exceed the white Asian heroin."

Knowings grinned. "You sure know your shit. You learn that in school or on the streets?"

"A little of both. It's like I keep telling you, Herm. You want to advance in this job, you have to take advantage of every opportunity to learn something that'll help you out."

Dunleavy's background and track record on the job lent her an air of credibility with Knowings on such matters. The daughter of a Westchester County orthopedic surgeon and a college professor, she had attended private schools and an Ivy League college. Her parents were initially disappointed, and a bit concerned, when she told them as a sophomore in college that she was planning on a career in law enforcement, abandoning her earlier plan to follow in her mother's footsteps into medicine. But by then they knew better than to attempt to talk her out of something she had her mind set on. Dunleavy interviewed with both Homeland Security and the FBI during her senior year in college, but ultimately she decided to join the New York City Police Department. Whereas many street cops hoped to make detective someday, Dunleavy aspired, at a minimum, to reach the level of department chief. Only three and a half years into the job, Dunleavy had already made sergeant and was attending law school at night. She was unapologetically ambitious, with a bit of a taste for the finer things in life, and seemed well on the way to fulfilling her professional aspirations.

Knowings's background was more typical for a New York City cop. Raised in the Astoria section of Queens, he came from a working-class—though by no means poor—family. His father drove a city bus, and his mother was a nurse's aide at the high school Knowings attended. Knowings was a good basketball player in high school and had a few Division II colleges sniffing around, but no scholarship offers materialized. With that path foreclosed, Knowings joined the army out of high school. His older brother was a New York City cop, which seemed like a viable career option for Knowings, so he signed up for MP training and spent four years as an MP, mostly in Afghanistan. He joined the New York City Police Department shortly after his discharge from the army. In his eighteen months on the job, he had already received two meritorious police duty medals and was highly regarded within his precinct.

* * *

Roughly two hundred miles northeast of Fort Greene, sixty-one-year-old Romero Matricula was doing what he liked to do best—eating. A heavyset, balding man sporting a bad comb-over, Matricula was talking business with his most trusted capo over lunch at Varano's, his favorite restaurant in Boston's North End. Originally settled in the 1630s, the North End was Boston's oldest neighborhood—and one of its most distinctive. From the late 1800s until the late 1900s, the area's residents were predominantly Italian American, which spawned the two features for which the North End was best known: a plethora of Italian restaurants and the headquarters of Massachusetts organized crime.

    In the fifteen-year period since the Antonino brothers were sent to prison, a rotating cast of characters laid claim to the title of underboss in Boston. No one lasted more than a few years. A few were replaced by the Salvaggio family, still overseeing things in New England; two wound up in federal prison; and one fell prey to another mobster looking to move up the ranks. Matricula had been underboss for a little more than a year. He rose to that position largely on his reputation for violence and ruthlessness; the Salvaggios thought he was the right person to keep a lid on any festering discontent in the Boston area. Matricula had no qualms about taking a guy out—particularly if the Salvaggios told him to. However, due to his somewhat limited intelligence and his lack of attention to detail, he proved to be less than the ideal person to be running things in the greater Boston area.

    By the time Matricula ascended to underboss, the turmoil in the leadership ranks had significantly diminished the sphere of influence of the Boston area underboss. The guys running things in Worcester and Springfield no longer answered to Boston; instead, they now paid tribute directly to the Salvaggios. And the unrest and internecine feuds among the crews operating in eastern Massachusetts and southern New Hampshire continued on Matricula's watch. He occasionally tried to quell discontent with a beating or killing. But this met with only limited success because he sometimes chose his targets unwisely, and he lacked the personality to galvanize the troops under him.

One of the crews operating under Matricula's umbrella was Spinelli's. Matricula wasn't quite sure what to make of Spinelli. On the one hand, he was like a bull in a china shop, and Matricula sometimes had to put out fires caused by Spinelli's aggressive tactics. On the other hand, Spinelli's various criminal enterprises took in a lot of money, and the slice of that flowing upstream into Matricula's pockets was not insubstantial.

"How much you get from Spinelli this week?" Matricula asked his capo.

"Just under three grand."

"Not bad. Last summer we were barely gettin' two grand a week outa him. What're you hearing about his business?"

"I'm hearing he's supplying most of the smack north of Boston. And that he just put a guy up in Manchester to deal there too."

"So he's expanding his territory?" asked Matricula.

"Looks that way."

"He playin' nice with our other crews?"

"Not really. From what I hear, he's dealin' and takin' bets in cities where we already got guys."

"Hmmm. That could cause some problems."

"You want me to have a talk with him, slap him down a little?" asked the capo.

"No, let him do his thing. We're takin' in more from him than any other guy we got out there. It ain't broke, don't fix it."

Chapter 19

As Dunleavy and Knowings sat talking just after noon, the radio in their squad car crackled to life. It was a heads-up from one of the detectives that they were about to raid the restaurant. The next contact came ten minutes later.

"Suspect just left the restaurant through the front door. White male in his twenties, five ten, medium build. Wearing jeans, a gray hooded sweatshirt, and a red backpack."

"You get the owner?" asked Dunleavy while Knowings started the car.

"Yeah, we got him, alright. You should see all smack he's got back here." Dunleavy could hear the smile in his voice.

Knowings eased the car slowly down the street in front of Mel's as he and Dunleavy scanned both sides of the street. "Got him," exclaimed Dunleavy. "Right side of the street, walking away from us." She pointed at Ryan Cunningham, walking briskly down the sidewalk.

"I see him," Knowings replied as he started to accelerate.

"No, hang back," Dunleavy ordered. "Wait for him to get in a car."

"What if he heads down into the subway?"

"These are out-of-town buyers, according to the narcotics guys. I'll bet he's got a car around here."

Knowings inched the car along for another thirty seconds, half a block behind Cunningham, before Cunningham stopped at a beat-up Toyota Corolla, unlocked the front door, and got in. Knowings continued to hang back.

"Move in now?" asked Knowings.

"Let him get a couple of blocks away, then pull him over," Dunleavy replied.

Cunningham pulled out into traffic, heading north on Carlton Avenue. He didn't know exactly where he was going, but he knew he needed to get on the Brooklyn-Queens Expressway, and his phone told him that was a few blocks north. The elevated expressway was in sight, and he was searching for signs directing him to an on-ramp when he heard the siren and noticed the flashing lights in his rearview mirror. For a fleeting second he thought about running, but he immediately realized he didn't even know how the hell to get out of that neighborhood. Slamming his hand on the steering wheel and shouting "Fuck me!", he pulled over.

Cunningham stopped just short of the entranceway to an alley, where he double-parked, partially blocking traffic. Using the car's external loudspeaker, Dunleavy ordered him to slowly pull into the alley just in front of him, which Dunleavy knew was a blind alley with no other egress. Knowings then pulled in behind Cunningham's car.

Dunleavy and Knowings approached the Corolla on opposite sides. Their guns weren't drawn, but their holsters were unsnapped, and they both had their right hands resting on the handles of their service revolvers. Knowings ordered Cunningham out of the car, frisked him, and checked his ID. Holding on to Cunningham's driver's license, he walked Cunningham to the front of his car and ordered him to lean forward, placing his hands spread apart on the hood. Dunleavy, meanwhile, was checking the car.

Stuffed under the front passenger seat was the red backpack Cunningham had been wearing when he'd exited Mel's. Dunleavy removed the backpack, opened it, and found a package covered with brown paper and heavily secured with clear packing tape. She sliced open the top of the package with a pocketknife, revealing a dark, brick-like substance, not unlike a lump of coal. After using her fingernail to scrape free a small fragment of the substance, Dunleavy tasted it and then smiled.

"Whatta we got there, partner?" asked Knowings, standing behind Cunningham.

"Those narco guys were right; it's black-tar heroin. It looks like half a key." Half of a kilo was a little more than a pound.

Looking at Cunningham, she asked, "What did you pay for this? I'm guessing thirty grand?"

Cunningham glared at her. "I'm not saying nothing till I talk to a lawyer."

Dunleavy looked at Knowings and smiled. "Do you think he's going to need a lawyer?"

"I don't think so," replied Knowings, grinning.

Cunningham was perplexed but remained silent.

"Did you give your cousin a heads-up that we might have something for him today?" Dunleavy asked.

"Sure did."

"Same price as last time?"

"Pretty much," said Knowings. "He said he'd give us thirty-five for a key, twenty for a half key, as long as the purity was about the same."

"I'm betting the purity of this stuff will be better than the last stuff we sold him."

"We gonna swing by his place now?"

"Yeah. Give him a call, tell him we'll be by in fifteen minutes."

Cunningham's mind was racing. What the fuck was going on here?

Dunleavy popped open the trunk of their patrol car, rearranged some gear back there, and placed the package of heroin underneath a canvas bag holding some tools. Closing the trunk, she looked at Cunningham and said, "You're free to go, Mr. Cunningham." Turning to Knowings, she said, "I don't think those narcotics guys will be *too* disappointed we weren't able to find the buyer after he left Mel's."

"Not with the bust they made, they won't," replied Knowings.

Knowings returned Cunningham's license to him and then turned and opened the front door of the squad car. Dunleavy was already in the passenger seat, looking impatient.

It was just dawning on Cunningham that he was being robbed. He suddenly realized that he was frightened more by that than by being arrested. "What are you guys doing?" he blurted out. "You can't do that!"

Knowings paused for a second before ducking into the car, a big grin on his face. "What're you gonna do, call the cops and tell 'em somebody stole your drugs?"

Chapter 20

The blood dripping from the cut below Ryan Cunningham's left eye was slowly forming a small pool on the linoleum floor of Jimmy O'Heir's kitchen. It was Friday night, and Cunningham was sitting in a chair, leaning forward with his head cradled in his hands. A scowling O'Heir was seated in a chair facing Cunningham. Standing to the side was Ernesto Fernandez, wiping some blood off his right fist.

"Tell me one more time how it happened," O'Heir snarled. Cunningham took a moment to compose himself and then repeated the story of how two New York City cops had stolen the heroin from him. As he had during Cunningham's first two recountings of the incident, O'Heir repeatedly interrupted him, probing for details. He didn't really care about the particulars; he just wanted to see if there were any inconsistencies in Cunningham's story.

O'Heir, who fancied himself a good judge of people, eventually satisfied himself that Cunningham was telling the truth (though not before Cunningham absorbed a pretty good beating). That did nothing to alleviate the problem, however. Losing a package of heroin—for which they'd just paid $25,000—was not going to go over well with Spinelli.

After sending Cunningham on his way, O'Heir placed a call to Benevento and broke the news to him about Cunningham being robbed. "Now that bastard owes us over fifty grand," Benevento said.

"Listen, man, we gotta tell Vin about this. He's not gonna be fuckin' happy."

"You didn't tell him yet?" Benevento asked.

"Gimme a fuckin' break," said O'Heir. "It just happened this afternoon. Besides, maybe *you* should tell him. Cunningham's your problem."

"Whoa, whoa, whoa, whoa, whoa. What the hell you talkin' about? He was buying *your* dope from *your* supplier. This whole thing was your idea."

"*My* fuckin' idea?" O'Heir retorted. "I never even heard of that motherfucker until you came to me and said you had a stiff who needed to work down his debt!"

Benevento was beginning to backpedal. In a battle of wits, he was no match for O'Heir. "Yeah, well, I never told you to send him on a run by himself."

"We *always* send just one guy to make those buys. Besides, you think it woulda made any difference if there were two stooges in the car instead of one?"

"Well, I'm not gonna be the one who goes to Vinny with this. It was your dope he lost."

"How 'bout we tell him together?" suggested O'Heir.

"How 'bout you tell him?"

"OK, Carmine, you want me to tell Vin? Then I'm gonna tell him that it was your idea to use Cunningham for this, and it was your mope who fucked this up."

"Alright, alright, we'll tell him together. Jesus Christ. When you wanna do it?"

"Let's go see him tomorrow."

A thought suddenly occurred to Benevento. "You know, Vinny gave us the green light on using Cunningham for this. Remember, last Monday at his house?"

"Yeah, so what?"

"So, it's not just our asses on the line. He OK'd that plan, too."

O'Heir chuckled. "You *really* think he's gonna see it that way?"

* * *

It took only a quick look inside Vinnie Spinelli's townhouse to know that he was not married. He had tied the knot at a young age, but that had barely lasted a year. Permanently soured on marriage by his brief but unpleasant experience with it, he now satisfied his urges with late-night bar pickups or some of the classier hookers within his employ (which is not to say he didn't also do that during his ill-fated marriage). But all of those trysts were "away games"—he never entertained women at home. His townhouse was reserved for get-togethers— both business and pleasure—with the guys, and it was furnished and maintained accordingly.

There were two bedrooms on the second floor: his own, outfitted with simply a bed and a dresser, and a guest bedroom containing three mattresses on the floor, adorned with sheets, quilts, and pillows. The main floor had a kitchen; a dining area, which contained not a dinner table but a card table; and a living room with two couches, a bar, a huge flat-screen TV hanging on the wall, and empty bottles strewn on the floor. The unfinished, windowless basement contained only a table and a few folding chairs, along with a tool bench; some of Spinelli's more unpleasant business was conducted down there.

Seated in Spinelli's living room on Saturday afternoon, O'Heir and Benevento exchanged furtive glances. O'Heir had just told Spinelli about the robbery of Cunningham and was bracing for the explosion that was sure to come. But Spinelli sat impassively, saying nothing. When he finally did speak, he was composed and analytical, not the raging maniac O'Heir and Benevento were expecting.

"Alright, first thing we gotta do is get a new package from New York. If we don't re-up our guys in the next day or so, they're gonna run outa shit to sell. And the last thing we want is their customers going elsewhere for their dope."

O'Heir nodded, relieved. *Damn*, he thought, *I'm done trying to figure this guy out.*

"Jimmy, call your man down there, but use a burner phone. If that fuckin' kid got stopped by the cops, they might've been watching our supplier—they might've even busted him. Find out what's going on down there."

"What do we do if he did get busted?" asked O'Heir.

"If you can't reach him, or even if things just don't sound right with him, let me know. I'm gonna make a few calls, try to line up a backup plan. There's so much smack coming in from Mexico these days that we won't have any trouble finding another source."

"Alright, Vin, I'll call him soon as I get home. I got a burner back there."

"Now, Carmine, what the fuck do we do about this Cunningham kid?"

Benevento hesitated. He didn't know if Spinelli was asking whether they should kill him or asking about how to collect from him. "Whaddaya mean?"

"What the fuck do you think I mean? What's this kid owe us, fifty grand?"

"A little more, with the vig."

"Well, how the hell we gonna get our money?"

Benevento had spent much of last night thinking about exactly that. He had only one thought to offer. "I checked this kid out. He's really got no money. He's got a shit-ass job, hardly makes anything there. His family's no help—his mother's a hairdresser and his old man looks like he's got less fuckin' money than the kid. The only thing I can think of, is TJ tells me that Cunningham's always running his mouth about how he's friends with this big NHL player. Maybe Cunningham can touch him up for a loan."

"Who's the NHL player?" asked Spinelli.

"His name's Nick Sullivan."

"Nick Sullivan on the Red Wings?"

"I think so. You know who he is?"

"Hell yeah. He's a big fucking star. He's from New Hampshire."

"That sounds right, I think that's where Cunningham's from. He lives in Manchester now, but I think he grew up around there, too."

"Alright, give it a try. Sullivan's gotta be making a few million a year; he can afford to bail out his buddy. Make sure you tell Cunningham that if Sullivan doesn't spot him the money, we're gonna break both his fuckin' legs. I want him motivated when he talks to Sullivan."

"You got it, Vinny. I'll talk to him today."

After Benevento and O'Heir left, Spinelli continued to mull over the Cunningham-Sullivan situation. Benevento had been gone only a few minutes when Spinelli reached him on his cell phone and asked him to come back. Five minutes later Benevento walked through the front door.

"So what's up, Vin?" Benevento asked, taking off his overcoat.

"How well does Cunningham know Sullivan?"

"I got no fuckin' idea, Vinny. I just know that TJ tells me he talks about him like they're good buddies. But he could be fulla shit."

"Here's what I'm thinking, Carmine. I wanna try to use Cunningham to get Sullivan to throw a game."

"So you can bet on the other team?"

"No, I just don't like the Red Wings. Of course so I can fuckin' bet on the other team!"

"Wow, that'd be unbelievable."

"If we can do this, we'll make a fuckin' killing. And you know what's even better? I'll show those Salvaggios what kinda operation I run up here. I'm so sick of paying tribute to that brain-dead rat-fuck Matricula. If we pull this off, and let the Salvaggio guys make money on the game too, I bet they'll let me take out Matricula and start running things up here myself."

"You really think Sullivan'd do that, though? That's pretty serious shit we're talking about."

"I know, Carmine. It's kind of a long shot. But let's give it a fuckin' try. Let's find out how tight Cunningham and Sullivan really are. Maybe Sullivan'll do it to save Cunningham's ass."

"OK, Vin. I'll meet with Cunningham today."

Spinelli thought for a minute. He decided he wanted to deal with Cunningham directly so he could assess the prospects of getting Sullivan to do this and make sure Cunningham was properly incentivized when he talked with Sullivan. And, if this did work out, he wanted to make sure that he was the one who got the credit for setting it up.

"No, Carmine. Bring Cunningham here tonight."

Chapter 21

Benevento knocked on Spinelli's door just after eight thirty that Saturday night. Standing behind him, nervously shifting his weight from one leg to the other, was Cunningham. After waiting about a minute, Benevento had started to knock on the door again when Spinelli jerked the door open.

"Hey, Vinny," Benevento said in greeting. Spinelli ignored Benevento and stared appraisingly at Cunningham, who was still fidgeting and avoiding eye contact with Spinelli. Spinelli waited a moment until Cunningham finally met his eyes and then said, "Get your sorry, dope-losing ass in here."

After Benevento and Cunningham were both inside, Spinelli said to Benevento, "You wait here." Turning to Cunningham, he then wordlessly pointed toward the open door leading downstairs. Cunningham paused; then he took a few uncertain steps toward the basement doorway. Impatient with Cunningham's tentativeness, Spinelli shoved him hard from behind. Cunningham pitched forward, barely regaining his balance in time to keep from plunging down the stairs. He then descended the steps at a brisk pace, glancing fearfully over his shoulder.

The table in the basement had a chair on either side of it and three objects on top: a bottle of Jack Daniels, a small mirror with several lines of cocaine laid out on it (and some residue left behind by the already-snorted lines), and a hammer. Spinelli took one seat and pointed to the other.

"Sit," he snarled.

Spinelli stared at Cunningham for a while, just to raise the tension and make sure Cunningham was uncomfortable. He then did a shot of Jack. When he finally spoke, his voice wasn't raised, but it radiated intensity and menace. "You owe us a lot of fuckin' money."

"I'm really sorry about the heroin. Those goddamn cops—"

"Shut the fuck up," Spinelli interrupted him. "I'm not interested in talking about how you got so far in the hole with us. I wanna talk about what you're gonna do to get out of it."

Cunningham started to say something, but Spinelli just held up his hand. "This is your lucky day, because I've already figured out how you're gonna pay us back. This is what you're gonna do. You're gonna get your buddy Nick Sullivan to throw a hockey game for us. You do that, all your debts'll be considered paid up."

"Throw an NHL game?" Cunningham asked incredulously.

"That's right, throw the game. The Red Wings play the Bruins up here on a Saturday night in a couple a weeks—that's the game I want him to dump. I'm gonna bet a boatload of fuckin' money on the Bruins that night. And I wanna be there to see this go down."

Cunningham was still stunned. He had spent the last hour, ever since Benevento called him, conjuring up a host of different scenarios that might unfold here tonight. This was not one of them. "I don't know, Mr. Spinelli, I haven't talked to Nick in years. We're really not friends anymore."

"That's not what TJ tells me. He says you're always talkin' about how Nick's your guy, how you guys are so tight."

"I told TJ we grew up together, how we were best friends in high school. I never said we were still friends," Cunningham whined.

"Were you really good friends in high school?"

"Yeah, I swear. We went to St. Xavier together. I played hockey with him there. We were good friends from the time we were little kids right through high school."

"When's the last time you talked with him?"

Cunningham expelled some air, thinking. "Shit, I don't know. Maybe seven, eight years ago?" Cunningham paused. "Maybe I could get him to lend me some money. Ya know, to pay you guys back."

Spinelli erupted, shouting at Cunningham. "No, you fuckin' moron! I want him to fix this game! I wanna show those guys in New York who should be runnin' things around here!"

Spinelli stared at Cunningham. It was time to up the ante a little. He picked up the hammer, leaned forward, and growled, "You better think of a fuckin' way to get him to do this. 'Cause if you don't, we're gonna drop you to the bottom of Boston fuckin' Harbor." He then brought the hammer down hard on Cunningham's right hand.

Cunningham yelped in pain, grabbing his right arm by the wrist. He was sure some of the bones there were shattered. The pain brought tears to his eyes, and it was a minute before he regained enough composure to speak. "How am I gonna get him to do that? Why would he do that?" The panic was now clear in Cunningham's voice, just as Spinelli intended. He wanted Cunningham to be desperate.

"Would he do this to save your ass, if you tell him we're gonna kill you if he doesn't do it?"

"Like I said, I haven't talked to him in a real long time. I don't think I can get him to do something like that for me."

"Well you better be real convincing," said Spinelli.

"I can try, man, I just don't think it's gonna work."

"Is there anything you can use? Does he owe you for something big you did for him when you were kids? Is there anything you can use against him?"

Cunningham suddenly thought of the fight in Kingsbridge Park ten years ago and the dead biker. Maybe he could get Nick to do it by threatening to tell the cops that he was the one who had killed that biker on the beach. Spinelli could see the wheels turning in Cunningham's head, and a glimmer of hope returned to him.

"You look like you thought of something you can use."

"Maybe. I got something that might work."

"What is it?"

Cunningham told him the story of how Nick accidentally killed a guy during a fight ten years ago, but one of their friends took the rap for him.

"So you think you can get Sullivan to throw the game by threatening to tell the cops the real story?"

"Maybe. I'll threaten him with the cops, or the newspapers, whatever," said Cunningham. "He's got a lot to lose if I do that."

"That's pretty fuckin' good, Cunningham. I like it. I want you to talk to him this week. I wanna move on this."

"OK, I can do that."

"You better make this work," said Spinelli. "'Cause I'm not fuckin' kidding about what we're gonna do with you if he doesn't do this."

Chapter 22

Owen Anderson returned to the conference room after a five-minute break, checking the pink phone-message slips his assistant had just given him. His clients—the chief financial officer and the general counsel of a fast-growing software company—were enjoying the stunning view of Boston Harbor and the North Shore afforded them by their perch thirty-two floors above Boston's bustling Atlantic Avenue. On this cold, clear Wednesday afternoon in January, the vista appeared to extend all the way up to the New Hampshire coast.

The three of them had spent over two hours plotting the strategy and timeline for the company's next round of fund-raising. They had been joined for the first part of their meeting by the lead Hart & Gates partner for this client, but he had excused himself forty-five minutes into the meeting. This pleased Owen for two reasons: he was gratified by the partner's display of confidence in him, and he was relieved that their efforts to actually get something accomplished would no longer be sidetracked by the partner's corny jokes and long-winded stories about similar deals he'd done.

As Owen flipped through his messages, he noticed two calls from Nick Sullivan—the first at 1:45 p.m., the second at 2:30 p.m., just fifteen minutes ago. Owen found that disquieting. Nick seldom called him at the office; when they did chat, it was usually at night or over the weekend. And two calls within an hour certainly indicated something was amiss. Potential scenarios were running through Owen's mind when his cell phone, set to vibrate during this meeting, buzzed. When he pulled it out of his suit coat pocket, he saw Nick's name on the caller-ID screen.

Owen's clients still had their backs to him, chatting and munching on chocolate chip cookies. Letting Nick's call go to voice mail, Owen approached the two men. After some brief small talk about the colossal LNG tanker inching through the harbor, Owen asked, "So, how do you think we're doing? Are we covering everything you wanted to?"

"Definitely—this is great," the CFO replied. "I had no idea there were so many moving pieces to a deal like this. But I'm feeling good about things."

"What do you think, Owen, about another hour to finish up here?" asked the GC.

"An hour tops. We can probably get through it in closer to half an hour. But listen, guys, I'm sorry, but I've just had something urgent come up. Can you give me another ten minutes or so before we get started again?"

"OK with me; I can return some calls," said the GC.

"No problem, Owen—that's fine," the CFO chimed in. "But could you have a few more of these cookies sent in?"

* * *

Owen hurried back to his office, tapping Nick's name on his iPhone to initiate the call as he was closing the door. Nick picked up during the first ring.

"Owen, thanks for calling back."

"What's up Sully? Is everything OK?"

"I got a problem, Owen. You're not gonna believe this one." The anxiety was evident in Nick's voice, but Owen stayed calm.

"I'm listening, Sully. What's going on?"

"You know who I just saw? Ryan Cunningham."

Owen's first reaction, having not heard from Cunningham in years, was to ask how he was doing. But one of the things he had learned in advising clients was that when someone had a problem, it was best just to listen for a while. He remained quiet, inviting Nick to continue.

Nick proceeded to fill him in on his call from Cunningham the night before and then their meeting earlier that afternoon. Nick relayed the story with more detail than was needed, and it became apparent to Owen that Nick was building up to something that he didn't really want to talk about. Other than an occasional prompt to keep Nick going, Owen silently let the story unfold. After describing Cunningham's trouble with some mob bookies, Nick finally got to the punch line.

"Owen, he wants me to throw a game."

Surprised but not shocked, Owen anticipated what was coming next. "And he says he'll tell the police about that night in Kingsbridge Park if you don't do it."

"Yes! Can you believe it? After all these years."

"Sully, there's no way you can throw a game."

"I *told* him no, Owen. And I know I shouldn't. That's risking my career. And I don't think I could do that to my teammates. But I really don't think he's bluffing about going to the cops. He seems pretty desperate."

Owen was thinking through the risks Nick was facing. He wasn't sure if, legally, Nick could still be charged with that death. But he understood that the publicity associated with even an unsuccessful prosecution could do irreparable damage to Nick's career.

"We can figure this out, Sully. We can find a way where you don't have to do this."

"Believe me, I want to. It just feels like I'm facing two horrible choices here. I'm really torn, Owen."

"Listen, give me a day or so to think this through. Don't say anything to Cunningham until then."

"He's probably gonna call me, Owen. He's not gonna just let this go."

"Don't answer. Or if you have to get back to him because he leaves some crazy, threatening voice mail, just tell him you're thinking about it. Just buy us a few days."

"Alright, I can do that."

"Let's see," Owen went on. "It's Wednesday afternoon. Where are you Friday and Saturday?"

"Montreal. We're playing the Canadians Saturday at one o'clock. We fly into Montreal Friday at around six or seven, I think."

"What hotel you staying at there?"

"I don't even know. We switch it up sometimes. I gotta check my travel sheet."

"That's fine; just text it to me. And let me know what time you're getting there. I'll meet you at your hotel Friday night."

"You're coming to Montreal?"

"Of course I'm coming to Montreal. We're gonna deal with this together, Sully."

Chapter 23

After finishing the meeting with his software clients, Owen retreated to the firm's research library, where phone calls and needy partners were less likely to intrude. With all the resources that were available on-line, the library was relatively modest in size and consisted primarily of cubicles and small rooms, where the firm's consultants could research or write in relative privacy, and reference desks manned by specialized research assistants. Owen planned to avail himself of both of those resources.

Owen first shut himself in a private room to think about the mess Nick had found himself in. He mentally explored a number of possible courses of action—some legal, some not. Each involved its own risks, and none seemed like a surefire solution. He did his best to analyze each approach objectively, assessing the likelihood of its success, the odds of its failure, and the magnitude of the toll that would be exacted—on Nick, on himself, or on someone else—if the gambit did fail. After about an hour, he settled on at least an initial approach. His confidence level in its success was not high, but he saw little downside to it. And if it didn't work, there was always a plan B.

Owen walked over to the area occupied by the research assistants, looking around for one in particular, a pretty, twentysomething redhead named Veronica. Veronica had proven herself to be very resourceful on other projects she had taken on for Owen. Just as importantly, she made it a habit to playfully flirt with Owen; he hoped her apparent affection for him would grease the skids on a request that required immediate attention. Owen spotted her engrossed in one of the three computer terminals on the semicircular desk in front of her.

"Hey, Veronica, how's it going today?" he said with a smile.

"Well, well, well, if it isn't Owen Anderson." She had a straight face, but there was a twinkle in her eyes. "I haven't seen you in here lately. Find someone who can service your needs better than I can?"

Owen upped the wattage on his smile. "That'd be impossible, Veronica. No one takes care of me like you do."

"Oh boy, I can feel a doozy of a request coming."

"Why do you say that?"

Veronica smiled for the first time. "Because men are so easy to read. Most of the time when you come in here, you're all business, usually in a hurry. No time for small talk with a flunky like me. But on those *rare* occasions you stoop to chitchatting with me, you always have some kind of special request—you need some research done right away, or you want me to run over to the Harvard Business School archives, or something like that."

"C'mon, Veronica, that's not true. You know I like talking with you."

"You're so full of shit, Owen," she said with a smile, clearly enjoying the fact that she had the upper hand in this conversation. "Stop wasting my time and just tell me what you need."

"Alright, Veronica. Next time I'm feeling social, I'll remember that you have no interest in talking to me." As she discreetly gave him the finger, he continued, "The firm uses private investigators from time to time, right?"

"Yeah, sure. We sometimes check into the backgrounds of executives at companies that our clients are considering doing business with."

"Who's the best one you've dealt with?"

"Oh, let's see…I've used about four or five different firms, and more than one guy—or woman—at each firm." She thought for minute. "I remember a guy who did some work for one of Jim Hennessey's clients a few months ago, and he did a great job. There was also another guy we used when one of our companies got caught up in that securities-fraud lawsuit that was brought against all those companies for how their IPOs were priced."

"Can you give me some names?" asked Owen.

"I don't remember them off the top of my head. I'm going to have to comb through my files."

"OK, can you do that for me Veronica? I need it pretty quickly, if you don't mind."

She was about to play hard to get, maybe make Owen grovel just a bit, but the hint of anxiety in his voice caused her to alter her approach. "Sure, Owen, I can deal with this other stuff a little later. I'll get back to you within about fifteen minutes."

Owen returned to his office and split his time between looking out the window and staring at the phone. He let two calls go through to voice mail before, ten minutes after he left Veronica, his phone chirped a third time, and he saw "Library" pop up on the caller-ID screen. He grabbed the handset.

"Veronica?"

"I've got two names for you, Owen. They're both very good, but I'd start with the first guy. He's worked wonders for us for two different clients."

Owen took down their names and contact information and then thanked Veronica profusely. He immediately dialed the number for her first recommendation, a guy named Jack Ludwick, who headed up his own investigative agency. His call went straight to voice mail, so he left a message, requesting a callback as soon as possible. He thought about calling the second name, but even though it was late in the day, he decided to give Ludwick thirty minutes before doing so. Pacing around his office had now replaced gazing out the window as his preferred means of attempting to make the time pass faster. He had just sat down to call the second investigator when he felt his cell phone, still on vibrate, buzz furiously. The caller ID read "Private caller."

"Hello, this is Owen Anderson."

"Jack Ludwick here."

"Hi, Mr. Ludwick, thanks for calling back."

"Call me Jack, please. You said you have an assignment for me?"

"I do, Jack, but first I want to talk with you about timing. This is an urgent matter, and I need to know if this is something you can turn to right away."

"Owen—may I call you Owen?—as you may know, I run an investigative firm with five other men working for me. I happen to be fairly occupied right now, but—assuming what you're looking for is up our alley—I can get one of my men to jump on it right away."

"Well, Jack, you personally come highly recommended. I'd really like you to handle this."

"May I ask where the recommendation came from?"

"Hart & Gates."

"Interesting. Hart & Gates is one of my top clients. I've got a lot of respect for some of the folks I do business with there. Do you work with Hart & Gates?"

After hesitating briefly, Owen said, "I'm an associate with Hart & Gates, but this isn't a firm matter, it's a personal matter."

"I see. Even if it's not a firm case, you're a Hart & Gates consultant, and I greatly value my relationship with Hart & Gates. I'd like to try and accommodate you if I can." He paused for a moment. "Why don't you tell me what it is you'd like us to do?"

Owen described what he needed.

"That's certainly within our bailiwick. It's possible this might even involve some travel. How about if I get one of my guys to do the legwork, but I stay involved in a supervisory capacity?"

"What would it take to get you to handle it directly yourself?"

There was silence for a minute. "Put yourself in the shoes of the client whose matter I'm currently handling. You wouldn't be happy if, in the middle of things, I turned that case over to someone else."

"You're right, I wouldn't be."

"I might actually lose that assignment," Ludwick went on.

Owen could see where Ludwick was leading him. "Would you take on my case personally if I pay you a premium above your normal fees?"

"What I'd need, to compensate for the risk of losing this other assignment, is for you pay twice my normal hourly rate."

"It's a deal. So long as you agree to work exclusively on my matter until you bring it to resolution."

Ludwick chuckled. "Do you even know what my rate is?"

"No, I don't, Jack. And I made it a point to agree to your request without asking that question, just to emphasize how important this case is to me."

"I understand, Owen. I want to get a little more information from you that might be helpful to me in this assignment. And it'll take about two minutes for me to cover some administrative stuff with you—our hourly rates, conflict of interest policy, stuff like that. Then, I give you my word, I'll get on your case as soon as we hang up the phone."

Chapter 24

It was just after four o'clock on Friday afternoon when Owen left the office. During the week he typically worked until at least seven thirty, but with the weekend beckoning, he tried to get out of the office by six on Fridays. Even for a Friday, though, a four o'clock departure was not easy to orchestrate. His primary obstacle was a due-diligence review meeting at four thirty. He told the partner on the deal that he needed to be out of the office at that time and asked whether it would be OK for him to participate by phone. Owen was relieved when she agreed without asking the reason for his absence.

Owen broke a few speed limits on the five-hour Boston-to-Montreal drive and arrived at the Red Wings' hotel at about eight thirty in the evening. The route took him directly through Pennington; he could see the spire of the St. Xavier chapel from the highway. This momentarily hijacked his thought process, as he spent some time thinking about his childhood, his childhood friends, and how their paths had diverged so wildly. He eventually snapped out of that reverie and returned to a dispassionate analysis of Nick's situation and the best way to handle it. By the time he walked into the hotel lobby and boarded the elevator to Nick's floor, his plan—built on the back of Jack Ludwick's work—had solidified.

After a quick embrace, Nick and Owen retreated to the sitting area of Nick's spacious hotel room. Owen discreetly sized up Nick's mood and could tell right away how tense Nick was. Owen had once visited with Nick two hours before the faceoff of a Stanley Cup finals game and found him to be completely relaxed, almost serene. But the current situation had clearly unnerved him.

Beyond the exchange of a few perfunctory texts, Owen and Nick had not been in touch with each other since their phone call on Wednesday afternoon. Eschewing any small talk, Owen dove right in.

"OK, Sully, I think I've got a plan. But first, have you heard from Cunningham since we last talked?"

"Yeah, he called me again yesterday. He wanted to know if I changed my mind."

"What'd you tell him?"

"I said I was thinking about it. Then I told him I couldn't believe what a douche bag he was."

"How'd he take all that?" asked Owen.

"OK, actually. When I saw him the first time, I told him flat-out no. So he was probably encouraged that I was at least thinking about it. He pressed me a little for an answer, and I said I'd let him know next week. That's still like ten days or so before the Bruins game." Nick paused momentarily. "There was no reaction to the douche-bag comment—I guess he already knows he is."

"You're probably right about that."

"Unbelievable, huh? To think that a guy you were friends with for most of your life would do this to you." Nick shook his head.

"He's not the same guy we knew, Nick. I don't know what the hell happened with him, but that's not the Ryan Cunningham we grew up with."

"I guess. Still…" Then, perking up a bit, Nick asked eagerly, "So, you said you had a plan?"

"I do. You ready for this?"

"Let's have it, man."

"I talked to someone who I think is gonna make this whole thing go away. Take a guess who."

"Stop busting my balls, Owen," Nick protested, but he was smiling. "Just tell me what's going on."

"I had a really good call last night with Dante Lombardo. He's gonna come back here and do whatever we need him to do to defend his story of what happened that night."

* * *

Jack Ludwick didn't start work on Owen's project—finding Dante Lombardo—as soon as he got off the phone with Owen, as he had promised. It was almost dinnertime by then, and Ludwick had plans, so he put it off until Thursday morning. He had no qualms about taking a somewhat cavalier approach to a seemingly urgent matter, though, because he was confident it wouldn't take him too long to locate Lombardo. In assessing this situation, Ludwick felt he had two things working in his favor, in addition to his abundant experience, that should make it relatively easy to track down Lombardo. One was

Owen's belief that Lombardo was in Arizona or New Mexico; narrowing the search area was always a huge plus. The second was that this didn't appear to be the case of someone who had actually gone into hiding. True, Lombardo had cut off contact with friends and family back in New England, but there was no reason to think he was using a different name or otherwise taking affirmative steps to conceal his whereabouts. Ludwick, of course, did not mention that to Owen. It was tough enough to justify the fees he was charging without telling Owen this wasn't a particularly difficult assignment.

In addition to the numerous free websites and search tools, Ludwick's firm subscribed to a variety of sophisticated record-retrieval services. Ludwick typically made use of both, as he often found what he was looking for using free search services—especially as he knew which ones were the best. As was his customary practice, he began by searching obituary records. If someone had died, there was almost always a public record of that. Besides, learning upfront that the target of your search was dead could avoid the time and money associated with what sometimes turned into exhaustive searches of the records of the living.

After the obituary searches turned up nothing, Ludwick progressed through the other databases he usually checked, including phone directories, state marriage and divorce records, registries of motor vehicles, and arrest records. As was usually the case, his searches turned up several false positives—that is positive results that were unhelpful to his search. For example, he found Lombardo's Rhode Island marriage license, two Rhode Island speeding tickets issued to him, and a misdemeanor citation for public intoxication in Central Falls, Rhode Island. But all of that had taken place before Lombardo dropped out of sight roughly two years ago.

Ludwick's first useful hit came about an hour and a half into his search—a Dante D. Lombardo, same date of birth as the search target, was arrested for disorderly conduct, apparently stemming from a barroom fight, in Hobbs, New Mexico, just three months earlier. After a few more searches of phone directories, real-estate files, and utilities records, Ludwick had a phone number and an address for Lombardo. As Ludwick dialed Owen's number to report his findings, two thoughts crossed his mind. One, it was really hard to disappear in this technological age. Two, if people knew how easy it was to do what he had just done, half of his business would evaporate.

* * *

Owen waited until eight thirty that night, six thirty New Mexico time, before calling Dante. He was pleased that Ludwick had given him a cell-phone number for Dante—Dante did not appear to have a landline at his apartment—which should increase the odds of actually getting through to him. Owen called from his cell phone. As Dante would not have Owen's cell number in his contacts, Owen believed—though he wasn't certain—that this meant his name would not appear on Dante's caller-ID screen. He was ambivalent about that—he wasn't sure whether seeing it was Owen calling would increase or decrease the chances of Dante's taking the call.

Owen's first two calls went straight to voice mail; he did not leave messages. His third call, placed shortly after nine o'clock, was answered with a brusque "hello." Owen wanted to believe that he recognized Dante's voice, but deep down he wasn't sure whether he did.

"Dante?"

"Who's this?" The tone was surly.

"Owen Anderson."

After a brief pause came a much softer reply. "Is that you, Owen?"

"It's me, Dante. How you been, man?"

This time the pause was longer. "Shit, Owen, you're not calling to see how I've been."

"You're right, Dante. That isn't why I called. But that doesn't mean I'm not interested in how you're doing. What've you been up to? Are you doing OK?"

"Depends what you mean by OK, I guess. I'm working right now, I got a place to live, the sun was out today. Things could be worse."

"How long've you been out there? I tried getting in touch with you when you were in Rhode Island."

In no mood to rehash the dispiriting course his life had taken over the last several years, Dante replied, "If you really want to hear my life's story, I'll tell it to you sometime. But let's start with this. How'd you find me? And why are you calling now, after all this time?"

"I hired a private investigator to track you down."

"No shit! You've had someone following me?"

"No, no, this guy just did a bunch of online searches and he was able to find an address and phone number for you."

"Are you serious? Some guy two thousand miles away found me by just sitting on his ass in front of his computer?" He chuckled. "I hope my wife doesn't know you can do that."

"So you wanna talk about why I'm calling?" asked Owen.

"Sure do."

"I need a favor from you."

"I figured as much," said Dante.

"Why do you say that?"

"Every time my phone rings, it's someone looking for something. The landlord's looking for rent, the Red Cross wants blood, the guy upstairs wants me to turn down my music, some politician I never heard of wants me to vote for him. I can barely take care of myself, and everyone else wants me to do something for them." His tone wasn't rancorous, just perplexed.

"Dante, I'm sorry to have to ask you this. Especially when I haven't talked to you in so long." Owen genuinely felt bad, not only for what he was about to ask, but for the tough life that Dante had apparently been living.

"It's about Sully, right?"

"It is. But how did you know?"

"C'mon, Owen. What other reason could you have to track me down?"

Owen told Dante about Cunningham's attempt to blackmail Nick into throwing a game. Dante was incensed. Although he had chosen, for a complicated set of reasons, not to stay in touch with Nick, he still took a certain amount of pride in Nick's success—due in no small part to his belief that Nick would not have had an NHL career if Dante hadn't taken the fall for Nick for the Kingsbridge Park incident.

"That fuckin' prick. I can't believe he'd do that to Sully."

"Yeah, it's a bad situation. I keep telling Sully he can't throw a game. But I can tell he's waffling. He's really afraid of Cunningham going to the cops or the media."

"So what do you want me to do, Owen? I'm sure you've got a plan. You always do."

Owen laid out his request. He wanted Dante to come back east; Nick would pay for his flight. Nick would arrange to meet with Cunningham, and Owen and Dante would show up at that meeting. The plan was for Dante to tell Cunningham that if he tried to tell anyone Nick was responsible for the death of the biker that night in Kingsbridge Park, Dante would stick to his story and exonerate Nick. So Cunningham might as well stop trying to blackmail Nick, because he really had nothing to threaten him with.

"What happens if Cunningham goes public with the story anyway? He sounds pretty desperate."

"Then you'd follow through and tell the police, or the press, or whoever, the same story you told ten years ago. Are you OK with that?"

"Sure. I got nothing to lose—I already took the rap, did the time for this. It's not like they can send me to jail again for the same thing." He paused momentarily. "You think that'll work?"

"Yeah, I do, Dante. That should get Nick off the hook. People are going to believe Nick and you, not a guy like Cunningham."

"Owen, I *am* a guy like Cunningham."

"You're not, Dante. You may have hit some rough patches in your life. But Cunningham is threatening someone who he was friends with for years just to save his own ass. You did the opposite—you sacrificed yourself to save a friend."

"You make it sound so noble, Owen. But let's not forget that what I did was lie through my teeth."

"Dante, if there's such thing as an honorable lie—and I believe there is—then that's what you told. The only person who was harmed by your story was you, and you were clearly willing to accept that. And you saved…you didn't save Sully's life, but you saved his career, and you made it possible for him to have the life he does. You should be proud of what you did, not ashamed of it."

"I'm not ashamed of it. But, I gotta tell you, there are days when I regret it."

"That's understandable, Dante. You gave up an awful lot. You did time in prison, and I know it's tough to get a decent job with that on your record." Owen paused. "Believe me, Sully feels bad about what you've gone through, and I do too. But Sully would have never asked you to do that, and he wouldn't have let you do it if he could've stopped you. All of this—the good you've done for Sully, the hardship you've brought on yourself—was strictly your call. You took a bullet for a friend. And you should be proud of that."

Chapter 25

Nick was sitting in a corner booth in the tastefully decorated tavern on the ground floor of the St. Regis Hotel in New York. It was noon on the Wednesday following his meeting with Owen in Montreal. The Red Wings were playing the New Jersey Devils that night at the Devils' home rink in Newark. As was their custom, the Red Wings stayed in Manhattan the night before the game. The team preferred the fifteen-mile bus ride from the St. Regis to the Prudential Center rink over staying in Newark. Downtown Newark had undergone somewhat of a revitalization in recent years, but Manhattan versus Newark was still no contest.

His eyes trained on the tavern entrance, Nick nervously awaited the arrival of Ryan Cunningham. A $500 tip to the maître d' ensured the tables to the left and right of Nick's booth would remain empty for the next forty-five minutes, guaranteeing them privacy for their conversation. The script was well rehearsed, but Nick was not certain it would work as planned.

Nick had called Cunningham on Sunday and told him he'd decided to throw the game against the Bruins. They agreed to meet for lunch today to work out the particulars. It was ten minutes after noon when Cunningham arrived at the tavern. Ignoring the hostess, he spotted Nick and strode over to the booth.

"What's up, Nick?" he said with a self-satisfied grin as he took a seat opposite Nick. Nick glared at him silently. "I'm glad you agreed to go along with this," said Cunningham. "This is gonna save both our asses."

Nick still did not respond. Cunningham was eyeing Nick warily when he was startled by someone sliding into the booth next to him. Not having seen him in ten years, it took a moment for Cunningham to recognize Dante. Nick could tell the precise moment when Cunningham realized who it was, as his smirk was instantaneously replaced by a stunned expression.

"Been a long time, Ryan," said Dante. "What's this I hear about you making up stories about Sully?"

After waiting a moment for Cunningham to absorb the import of Dante's presence, Owen walked over and sat down next to Nick. Dumbfounded by the appearance of Dante and Owen, Cunningham just stared at Owen. Owen returned the glare for a moment and then spoke in a low voice.

"There's been a change of plans, Ryan. This is how it's gonna work. Are you listening?"

Cunningham said nothing.

"Nick is not throwing the Bruins game. He was never even considering doing that. So you go back and tell your buddies that's not happening."

Cunningham glanced over at Nick, but Nick just glared impassively at him.

"If you tell anyone—the police, reporters, anyone—that Nick was responsible for what happened in Kingsbridge Park that night, Dante will go to whoever you talked to and tell them his story. And remember what he's got behind his story. The cops believed him. I backed up his story then, and I'll do it again. Even the biker who was there said it was Dante. Dante's fingerprints were on the chain that killed the guy. He pled guilty and did time for the killing. And we're even going tell people you're blackmailing Nick because you've got a big gambling debt you need to square. There is no way *in hell* that anyone will believe you. So don't even bother trying to sell that story. You'll end up looking like a lying asshole. And you still wouldn't have gotten Nick to do what you wanted."

"Shit, Owen, these guys'll kill me if Nick doesn't do this."

"Sully said you owed something like fifty thousand dollars," said Owen. "Even though you're a total prick for pulling this shit on Nick, he's still willing to talk to you about loaning you the money you need to get out from under this."

"We're past that, Owen," Cunningham whined. "These guys don't want just their money. This guy Spinelli wants to prove to some New York big shots that he can fix an NHL game."

Owen made a mental note of the name Spinelli. "That's just not going to happen, Ryan. If you need help with money, call me and I'll talk to Nick. Don't call Nick."

Nick spoke up for the first time. "We were friends a long time. I can't believe you tried to blackmail me into throwing a game. Don't ever call me again, about anything."

With that, Owen, Nick, and Dante stood up, leaving Cunningham still sitting at the booth. Before leaving, Owen looked back and said, "Dante's backing Sully on this. You've got nothing left to threaten him with."

Chapter 26

Shortly before ten o'clock on Thursday morning, in the throes of a raging hangover, Cunningham made the call he'd been putting off for almost twenty-four hours. He'd thought about placing the call following his unsettling encounter with Nick, Dante, and Owen the previous day, but he couldn't bring himself to do it. Instead, he bought a pint of Jack Daniels and gradually got drunk on his drive back to Manchester, ignoring two calls from Spinelli. Rather than returning home, he headed straight to a local pub, where he played some darts and threw back a few more shots. By eight o'clock that night, he was so drunk he was slurring his words, which provided him with a convenient excuse to delay the call until the next morning.

Spinelli picked up on the first ring. "Where the fuck you been? I tried calling you yesterday. When I fuckin' call you, you answer, you hear me?"

"Yeah, sorry 'bout that, Mr. Spinelli."

"How'd your meeting with Sullivan go?"

"Not so good," said Cunningham.

"What the fuck do you mean, 'Not so good'?"

Cunningham told him about Dante and Owen showing up at his meeting with Nick and promising to back up their original story.

"Slow down, slow down. Who the fuck is this Lombardo guy?"

"He's the guy who confessed to the killing and did time for it. He says he'll tell his same story to the cops, to reporters, whoever. He already did time for it, so he's got nothing to lose."

"I thought you said he'd disappeared, no one knew where he was."

"He did," said Cunningham. "He took off a few years ago, and no one around here had heard from him. But he's back now."

"And who's the other guy?"

"Anderson? He's some type of business guy in Boston. He's probably the guy who tracked down Lombardo."

"So Sullivan said he's not going do it?"

"That's right. He said if I tell anyone that he killed the guy, no one'll believe me with Lombardo sticking to his story."

"God fuckin' damn it!" exclaimed Spinelli.

Cunningham remained silent for a moment and then said, "You want me to go to the cops anyway, see what he does?"

After thinking about that briefly, Spinelli said, "No point. Our only leverage against Sullivan was threatening him, getting him to throw the game so you *don't* go public with your story. Once you do go public, there's no reason for Sullivan to throw the game."

Cunningham was afraid to ask what to do next. He thought the answer might be that Spinelli would simply kill him.

"I gotta think about this some more," said Spinelli after a moment. "Don't go anywhere, kid. You'll be hearing from me soon."

* * *

Earlier that same morning, Owen and Dante had grabbed a quick breakfast at a Faneuil Hall Marketplace diner, not far from Owen's condo—where Dante was staying—before Owen headed in to work. Although Dante had willingly interrupted his self-imposed exile to help Nick out, being back in New England had him feeling uncomfortable, out of his element.

"So how long are you planning to stay out here?" Owen asked over a plate of scrambled eggs and hash browns.

"How long you think I need to?"

"The Red Wings-Bruins game's a week from Saturday. If Cunningham is going to do anything, he'll do it by then. So I'd say at least until next Saturday."

"You think he's still gonna try to jam Sully up?"

"No, I don't think so. Now that he knows you'll stick to your story, there's really no point in it. Even if he's not smart enough to see that, I bet the mob guys who put him up to this are." Owen paused. "Still, can you stick around until then just in case?"

"That's not a problem. I think the restaurant where I work can survive with one less busboy for the next week." He laughed sarcastically. "Besides, I've probably already been fired."

"You know, Dante, you're welcome to stay beyond next Saturday. No one else is using my spare bedroom. You ought to think about moving back here."

"I don't know, Owen, I don't think that's such a great idea. I mean, I appreciate the offer and all. But I just don't see myself doin' that."

"You should really think about it, Dante. You grew up here, you still have friends here." A pause. "You've got family here now too." Owen had told Dante about his daughter—now eighteen months old—the night before.

"Look, Owen, I'm gonna go see my daughter before I go back," said Dante. "And it's been good to see you and Sully again, even under shitty circumstances. But being back here is mostly bad memories. My mom's dead, my old man's gone...and I didn't exactly have a great relationship with him when he was around. If I had to do it all over again, I'd still take the hit for Sully. But that year in jail isn't something I like to think about. My marriage was a train wreck. I got a kid who doesn't even know who I am. Being around here just reminds me of a whole bunch of things I'd rather not think about."

For once, Owen found himself at a loss for words.

* * *

Spinelli called Cunningham back early that afternoon. Afraid of what he might hear, Cunningham didn't answer the first call. When Spinelli called again two minutes later, Cunningham decided not to risk pissing Spinelli off further by not picking up.

"Hello."

"Where are you?"

"I'm at my apartment, getting ready to go in to work."

"Alright, just checking. If you take off anywhere, I'll know about it. Listen, you know where that Lombardo guy is?"

"No," said Cunningham.

"He must still be around here, right? If he said he'll tell everyone you're full of shit if you blow the whistle on Sullivan, he must still be around."

"I guess."

"Fuckin' work with me here, Cunningham," said Spinelli. "Where would he be staying? He got family here?"

"I don't think so. His mother died when he was a little kid, and I think his father moved away."

"Who else would he stay with? The other fuckin' guy? What's his name—Anderson?"

"That could be. They were always good friends. And like I told you, it was probably Anderson that found Lombardo and brought him back here."

"Why do you say that?"

"Because he's always doing shit like that," said Cunningham. "You know, plannin' things, fixin' things."

"OK, you know where Anderson lives?"

"I'm pretty sure he lives in Boston—like, right in the city."

"Where's he work?"

"I don't know the name of the company. But it's a big-name place. I bet if you Google his name, his company's name'll come up."

Spinelli thought for a moment. "What's Anderson's middle name?"

"Man, I know this. It was a last name, not a first name, ya know? Lemme think...Callahan! Yeah, Owen Callahan Anderson. I think that was his mother's name."

"Good. And how old is he?"

"Same age as me, our birthdays are like a month apart," said Cunningham. "So twenty-eight."

"Alright, that should give me enough to find out where Anderson lives. I'll be in touch."

Chapter 27

Ernesto Fernandez was slouched in the driver's seat of his black Ford Explorer midmorning on Friday, debating whether to start the engine and turn on the heat. Though wearing a heavy winter jacket, ski gloves, and a wool hat pulled down over his ears and just above his dark sunglasses, he was freezing his ass off on this cold winter morning. But he knew the risk of attracting attention to himself was greater if the car was running, so he dutifully resisted that temptation. He promised himself another cup of hot coffee before noon and kept his eyes trained on the red door twenty yards down the street.

Fernandez was parked on Grove Street in Boston's fashionable Beacon Hill neighborhood. Beacon Hill was sandwiched between the Charles River and the Boston Common, within walking distance of several Boston hotspots, including the financial district, Faneuil Hall Marketplace, the North End, and the Back Bay. After renting a nearby studio apartment for the first eighteen months after he'd joined Hart & Gates, Owen had purchased a small but tasteful two-bedroom condo on Grove Street just over a year ago. It was the entrance to that condo building that Fernandez had been watching since just before seven o'clock that morning.

The front entrance to Owen's building afforded access to a total of six condos in that three-story building, so some of the foot traffic in and out of the building was of no interest to Fernandez. He was watching for only two people—Owen and Dante. He saw Owen leave the building at about seven thirty that morning, presumably heading for work. Spotting Owen had been easy, as Fernandez was armed with a recent picture of him obtained from the Hart & Gates website. Recognizing Dante could be a little trickier. All he had on him was a description from Cunningham and a ten-year-old mug shot. So far that morning, besides Owen, three guys who left the building looked to be around the right age. But none of them looked much like the eighteen-year-old Dante. Just as telling, all had been dressed in what was clearly business attire. Fernandez was assuming Dante would be wearing more casual clothes.

At five minutes before noon, a man emerged from the building wearing jeans, sneakers, and a black North Face jacket. Fernandez looked at him intently, believing it could be Dante. The man walked away in the opposite direction from Fernandez's parking spot, though, depriving Fernandez of a good look.

Fernandez immediately hopped out of the Explorer and closed to within twenty feet of the man, following him as he walked down Grove Street and turned right onto the much busier Cambridge Street. The noontime foot traffic on Cambridge Street made it difficult for Fernandez to get a good look at the man, but he kept him in sight as he walked briskly up Cambridge Street toward city hall for about five minutes before ducking into a McDonald's. Fernandez followed him inside and got into line immediately to the left of his line, where Fernandez had a good view of him. This person matched the height and weight Cunningham had described, and his face bore a strong resemblance to the mug shot Fernandez had surreptitiously studied before entering the McDonald's. Fernandez was certain this was Dante Lombardo.

Fernandez followed him back to Owen's condo, where he disappeared with his bag of McDonald's food behind the red door. After getting into his Explorer, Fernandez called Spinelli to let him know he had found Dante. He then listened carefully to the detailed instructions Spinelli laid out for him.

* * *

About an hour later, Billy Cundiff, wearing a black down jacket and a scarf covering most of his face, approached the Explorer from behind, quietly opened the passenger door, and slid into the front seat.

"Christ, Billy, you scared me, man!" exclaimed Fernandez.

"You didn't see me comin'?"

"I'm watching the fuckin' front door, not lookin' for assholes walking down the street."

"So what's the story? Lombardo still in there?"

"Yeah."

"Anyone else go into the building?"

"Not since Lombardo did about an hour ago."

"OK, let's run through it once. Then we'll head in."

Fernandez started the car and pulled up directly in front of Owen's building. Both men donned latex gloves. Befitting an early weekday afternoon on a quiet residential street, there was no one else in sight. As Fernandez stood watch, Cundiff quickly picked the lock to the front door of the building, and then both men stepped inside.

The layout of the building was simple. There were two condos on each floor, one to the left and one to the right of the stairwell leading up to the third floor. Owen's condo was on the second floor. Cundiff waited just inside the building's front door to warn Fernandez in the event anyone else entered, and Fernandez quietly ascended the staircase to the second floor. While Cundiff had no trouble picking the lock on the building's front door, Spinelli had instructed them not to attempt that on the door to Owen's condo; he worried the owners of the individual units were likely to have more secure locks and perhaps even an alarm system. Instead, Fernandez rapped lightly on Owen's door.

After a few seconds, Fernandez heard footsteps approach the door, followed by Dante asking, "Who's there?"

"Hey, Owen, it's Peter, from the third floor. I lost my key again. Can I grab the spare key you keep for me?"

After a brief pause, Dante replied, "Owen's not home. This is a friend of his."

"Oh, sorry to bother you, man. Owen has an extra key to my condo. I know where he keeps it. Can I just grab it?"

Dante's instinct was to tell the guy to get lost, but he didn't want to create trouble between Owen and his neighbors. He decided he wouldn't let the guy in to get his key, but he would let the guy tell him where it was so he could get it for him. Dante cracked the door open.

As soon as he did, Fernandez gave the door a violent kick, knocking it back into Dante. As Dante fell to the floor, Fernandez stepped inside and removed a black sap—a small but heavy leather-covered weapon, also known as a blackjack—from a pocket on the inside of his jacket. Before Dante knew what was happening, Fernandez struck him twice in the temple area, knocking him unconscious.

Fernandez then stepped out into the hall and motioned to Cundiff, one floor below. Cundiff retrieved a large army-green duffel bag from the Explorer and joined Fernandez inside Owen's condo. Extracting a small plastic tarp from the duffel bag, Fernandez placed it under Dante's upper body and folded it over so it covered his head. Fernandez then took a pistol—a SIG Mosquito equipped with an AAC Pilot silencer—out of the duffel bag and fired two shots into Dante's forehead, killing him instantly.

Fernandez quickly checked Dante's pockets, removing his cell phone (which he turned off) but leaving his wallet. Though it took a bit of effort, Fernandez and

Cundiff then stuffed Dante's body into the duffel bag. As they struggled with this task, Cundiff muttered, "Why the fuck can't we just leave him here?"

"I'm sure Vinny's got a reason."

"Don't make no sense to me."

"Next time they pay you to think, you let me know. Till then, let's just fuckin' do what we're told."

After satisfying themselves that no blood had splattered onto the rug and making sure there was no one in the stairwell, they carried the duffel bag down to the building's main entrance. A check of the street confirmed all was quiet there as well, and they quickly deposited the duffel bag in the back of the Explorer and covered it with a blanket. Thirty seconds later they were turning onto Cambridge Street and heading toward the Tobin Bridge, which would carry them out of town to the north.

It took about fifteen minutes of cruising the side streets around the Rumney Marsh Reservation straddling the border between Revere and Saugus before they came across a secluded spot with neither pedestrians nor cars in sight. Together Fernandez and Cundiff dumped the duffel bag at the edge of the marsh, and Fernandez then threw Dante's cell phone as far into the marsh as he could. As they drove away, Cundiff jotted down some notes on the precise location where they left the body. Fernandez then called Spinelli to report in.

Chapter 28

Nick was half asleep on the couch when he was startled awake by the ringing of his cell phone. It was almost two o'clock on Friday afternoon. He had just returned home from practice and was resting before going up to his bedroom for some much-needed time in the hot tub. Seeing "Unavailable" on the caller-ID screen, Nick rejected the call and gathered himself to head upstairs.

As he walked into his bedroom, Nick noticed the icon on his cell phone indicating a new voice mail. He found that slightly odd, as most of the calls he received from unavailable numbers were the verbal equivalents of e-mail spam and seldom resulted in voice-mail messages. Reminding himself for the umpteenth time since he'd foolishly given his cell number to Cunningham that he needed to change his number, Nick dialed his voice mail and listened to the message as he began to disrobe for the hot tub. Though Nick didn't know whom he was listening to, the gravelly voice of Vinnie Spinelli immediately grabbed his attention.

"Yo, Nick, this is a friend of Ryan Cunningham. I suggest you call your buddy Owen Anderson and ask him where his houseguest is. If he can't find him, tell him to check a spot at the edge of the marsh about twenty-five yards from where Bledsoe Street in Saugus dead ends. I'm gonna call you back at exactly five o'clock today. You better pick up that call."

Nick sat down on his bed, trying to digest the message he had just listened to. His first thought was that the guy might be bluffing, but he quickly dismissed that notion—if Dante wasn't at the spot described, the caller would have no more leverage or credibility. He then began to wonder whether Dante would have been left there alive or dead. Pushing that thought from his head, he replayed the message, writing it down word for word. He then called Owen's cell phone.

"Hey, Sully, what's up?"

"Owen, man, I think we got a problem."

"You sound a little shaken up, Nick. What's going on?"

"Some guy just left a voice mail on my cell. Lemme read it to you." He repeated the message for Owen.

Owen's voice was grim. "Sully, where are you—are you at home in Grosse Point?"

"Yeah."

"Listen, just sit tight. I've gotta check out some things on this end. I'll get back to you before five."

"Should I answer my phone if I don't recognize the caller?"

Owen thought for a moment. "This guy probably won't call back before five o'clock. If you do get any calls you don't recognize before then, let 'em go into voice mail. There's nothing to be gained right now by you saying anything to anybody about all this. Even if that same guy calls back, I don't think you'll piss him off by not picking up, as long as you take his call at five."

"And you'll get back to me before then?"

"I promise, you'll hear from me before five o'clock."

* * *

After failing to reach Dante on either his cell phone or his own home phone, Owen asked his assistant to reschedule the one meeting on his calendar for that afternoon and left the office to return to his condo. Finding it empty, he briefly looked around the place. Dante's small overnight bag, stuffed with a few changes of clothes, was still on the floor of the guest bedroom. There was no note and no obvious indication of a struggle or forced entry.

Owen debated whether he should call the police. On the one hand, any discussion with the police could eventually lead to a revisiting of the Kingsbridge Park incident, which Owen desperately wanted to avoid. On the other hand, Owen knew there was a real possibility that what lay at the edge of the Saugus marsh was Dante's body. Ultimately, he decided he needed to go to the police—he was almost certainly dealing with either a missing person or a murder, so the authorities would have to be brought into the picture. He did not, however, need to tell them the whole story. Above all, he wanted to keep Nick's name out of it.

Before making the twenty-minute drive from downtown Boston to the Saugus police station, Owen had one stop to make. He was in and out of a nearby

Walgreens in less than five minutes. After a quick phone call, Owen was on the road. He tried Dante's cell a few more times on the ride but again got only voice mail. Having already left two messages for him, Owen simply hung up.

At Saugus police headquarters, Owen met with a Sergeant Patterson after a five-minute wait. Patterson turned out to be a no-nonsense type of guy with a gruff manner. After brief introductions, Patterson asked, "So what brings you here today?"

"I think a friend of mine is missing. He's been staying with me, but he's not at my place and I can't reach him on his cell. And I received a strange message within the last hour that said I could find him at the Rumney marsh, near the end of Bledsoe Street."

Patterson took out a pen and began making some notes. "What's your friend's name?"

"Dante Lombardo."

"When did you last see him?"

"Early this morning, before I went to work."

Patterson put down his pen and sat back. "So he's only been missing a few hours?"

"Yes. Look, I don't even know for sure he's missing. But he's not at my condominium. He's not really from around here, so I don't know where else he'd be. I've tried about five times to get him on his cell phone, but he's not answering. And that message I got about him finding him at the marsh makes me think something strange has happened."

"Tell me about the message."

Though he knew it was coming, this was the one question Owen did not want to answer—the one question he would not answer truthfully. "I received a call about forty-five minutes ago. I don't know who it was from; the caller ID said 'unavailable.' A man's voice I didn't recognize said—this isn't an exact quote, but it's close—'I suggest you check on your buddy Dante Lombardo. If you can't find him, check a spot at the edge of the marsh about twenty-five yards from where Bledsoe Street in Saugus dead ends.'"

"So this wasn't a voice mail—you talked to this guy?"

"I didn't really talk to him. I said hello, and he said what I just told you and hung up. The call couldn't have last more than ten seconds."

"This call was made to your cell phone?"

"Yes."

"Do you have it with you?" asked Patterson.

"Yes, you want to see it?"

"If you don't mind."

Owen handed him his iPhone. Patterson checked the call log and saw one incoming call in the last hour, with a duration of eight seconds.

"This is the call right here?" Patterson asked, showing Owen the call log.

"Yeah, that's it," said Owen.

"And you don't recognize this number?"

"No." The number belonged to a prepaid cell phone Owen had bought at Walgreens. Owen knew he had to fabricate part of his story to avoid dragging Nick into this, and he also knew he had to create a record to support the story he planned to tell. So he bought the disposable phone and placed a call to his own cell phone from the Walgreens parking lot. He answered that call and then hung up after about ten seconds, creating an electronic trail to back up his story.

"Alright. Let's take a drive out to Rumney marsh. The caller said the end of Bledsoe Street?"

"Yes, that's right."

As they walked out to Patterson's squad car, Owen asked, "Do you know that area?"

"Yeah. There's a residential area just to the west of the Rumney Marsh Reservation. Bledsoe runs from Saugus center right down to the edge of the marsh. It ends in a dead end there."

On the ride, in response to a series of questions from Patterson, Owen provided more background on Dante. He recounted their childhood friendship and briefly described the struggles Dante had confronted in more recent years, including his failed marriage and his subsequent disappearance. Owen told Patterson that he recently had decided to try to find Dante, and that with the help of a private investigator he had done so. Some subtle hints Owen dropped about tough times Dante had encountered in New Mexico created room for speculation that Dante may have made a few enemies over the years.

Owen then related that Dante had, within the past week, returned east for a visit and was staying with Owen. That pretty much filled in the blanks up until the phone call Owen received—or said he received—earlier that afternoon.

Reaching the end of Bledsoe Street, Patterson pulled over and parked on the dirt shoulder. The edge of the water looked to be about thirty or forty yards away. After ten yards or so, the firm terrain gave way to knee-high grass sprouting from increasingly damp ground. With the grass obscuring their view, they trudged almost to the edge of the water before Patterson stopped and silently pointed to a large green duffel bag about ten feet to their left.

Owen, cursing under his breath, followed Patterson to the duffel bag. Patterson slipped on some gloves and unzipped the bag. Although the body was doubled over to fit in the duffel bag, Dante's face—and the two gunshot wounds in his forehead—were clearly visible. After Owen confirmed it was Dante, Patterson called the coroner and began cordoning off the scene with bright-yellow crime tape.

Chapter 29

The hours following his early afternoon call with Owen dragged by for Nick. He tried watching TV but gave up after an hour spent mindlessly staring at ESPN News or aimlessly flipping the channels. After thinking about going for a walk, he decided against it so he wouldn't have to take a call in a public setting. He eventually resorted to fidgeting with his phone—playing Candy Crush, checking Twitter. As he did so, he couldn't decide whether he wanted the phone to ring or not.

When his phone finally did ring at about four thirty, he was relieved to see Owen's name on the caller ID. That relief lasted only until he answered the call.

"Owen, what's going on?"

"Dante's dead."

"Goddamn it! I knew it!" After a few seconds, in a calmer yet still angry voice, he asked, "What happened?"

"He was shot in the head. Twice."

"Was he at that spot where the guy in the voice mail said he'd be?"

"Yeah, he was, Sully." Owen proceeded to fill Nick in on what had transpired since they'd spoken a few hours earlier. They then spent a few minutes reminiscing about growing up with Dante and their high-school years. Nick was getting emotional, and Owen could sense what was coming.

"This is my fault, Owen. This only happened because he was gonna go to bat for me. Again."

"That's just not true, Sully. Dante was a grown man, making his own choices. No one made him do anything. Shit, you didn't even *ask* him to back up your story. The only person who asked him to do anything was me. And I barely asked him anything—once I told him what was happening, right away he said, 'I got Sully's back on this. What do you want me to do?'"

Nick was silent. After a beat Owen continued. "What we gotta do now, Sully, is focus on what's going to happen, not what's already happened."

"You know what comes next, right? When my phone rings at five, they're gonna tell me I have to throw the Bruins game next Saturday. Without Dante, they can go back to their original threat—either I throw that game or Cunningham goes public with his story."

"Sully, you still gotta tell them no. I'll stick to the story I told the cops ten years ago—it was an accident, but it was Dante, not you."

"Shit, Owen, I don't like this. I don't want you to have to lie again for me. And I *know* you don't want to be pointing the finger at Dante when he's not around to stick up for himself."

That struck a nerve with Owen. But he could sense Nick's resolve wavering, so he pressed on. "C'mon, Sully. You know Dante would want me to do that. He's the one who came all the way back here just to stick to his story and keep you out of this."

"I'm just not feelin' so good about this now," said Nick. "These assholes have their leverage back, and they know it."

"Not really, Nick. I think people are gonna be more likely to believe me than Cunningham."

"Maybe you're right about that. But let's say I don't end up going to jail over this. My career'll probably still be screwed. There's definitely gonna be people who do believe Cunningham. And I'm a free agent after this year, Owen. You think a lot of teams'll wanna sign me after all that negative publicity?"

"We just have to convince everyone that Cunningham's full of shit," said Owen. "We can do that, Sully."

"You sound pretty sure of that. But remember, Cunningham's gonna be the one telling the truth."

"We can do this, Nick. You just gotta stay strong. Trust me, we're gonna get through this."

"Alright, man, thanks for being there for me on this. I gotta run. That prick's gonna be calling me back in a couple of minutes."

"OK, call me back as soon as you get off that call."

*　*　*

It was precisely five o'clock when Nick's cell phone rang again. Nick immediately recognized the caller as the scumbag who had left the voice mail a few hours earlier.

"So Nick, have you talked to your pal Owen?"

After a brief pause, Nick replied, "Yes."

"So you know what happened to Dante Lombardo?"

"Yes."

"I think you can see, Nick, I'm not the kinda guy you wanna fuck with. You unnerstan'?"

Silence.

In a louder voice, Spinelli repeated, "I *said*, do you understand?"

"Yes."

"Maybe your lowlife friend Cunningham didn't deliver my message clearly. So I'm gonna spell it out for you. You make sure you lose to the Bruins next Saturday. If you do, we all go on our merry way, you'll never hear from me again. If you don't play along with this, Cunningham tells the story of what really happened ten years ago at that beach in Kingsbridge Park. How it was you who killed that guy, not Lombardo. His first call is to that guy Ted Cusack who covers the Red Wings for the *Detroit Free Press*. His second call is to the Belknap County DA—I got his name and number right here. Yeah, Nick, we done our homework on this. Next he calls ESPN. That ought to be enough to guarantee you're fucked, one way or another."

He paused for dramatic effect. "So, what's it gonna be, Nick? You in or you out?"

Nick tried to sound resolute, though he certainly wasn't feeling that way. "I need some time to think about this. I'll let you know tomorrow."

"OK, Nicky. But here's two more things for you to think about when you lay your little head down on that pillow tonight. First, if we don't hear a yes from you by tomorrow, Cunningham starts making his calls and telling his story on Sunday. Second, there's more to Cunningham's story. You wanna hear the rest?"

Nick didn't respond.

"Cunningham's also gonna tell everyone that he'd been talking to Lombardo in the last couple of weeks. That Lombardo told him he called you, asking for a little help to get him through some tough times he was having. And when you acted like a big-time asshole star and told him no, he got pissed and told you he was gonna blow the whistle on you and clear his name after all these years. Then he called Cunningham and told him what he was planning to do, and Cunningham agreed to help Lombardo out by backing up his story. Now the way I see it, Nicky, that does two things for us. One, hard as that is to do, it makes Cunningham look like the good guy here. He's not just some bitter guy trying to screw an old friend. He's sticking up for his poor murdered buddy and trying to finally clear his buddy's name. And the second thing, Nick, is even better. The cops right now have no idea who killed Lombardo. But once Cunningham tells that story, it's gonna be pretty clear who had a motive to kill Lombardo. Maybe you can prove you weren't in Boston when it happened, but what about your friend Anderson? I'll bet the cops take a long, hard look at him."

Nick was speechless.

Spinelli concluded the call by saying, "I'm gonna call you tomorrow afternoon. You better fuckin' tell me what I wanna hear."

Chapter 30

Owen returned to his office at five thirty on Friday evening, needing to catch up on some work that had languished due to his periodic absences over the last week. His progress was impeded by his wavering concentration, as at least half his time was spent pondering Nick's situation, trying plot the right course of action. He was growing anxious about not hearing from Nick when his cell phone rang a few minutes before six o'clock.

"Sully, what's going on? Did the guy call back?"

"Yeah, I just hung up with the bastard." In fact, Nick had gotten off the phone with Spinelli shortly after five o'clock. But he had put off his call to Owen, debating what he was going to say to him.

"So what happened? What'd he have to say?"

"Same ol' shit. He wants me to throw the Bruins game next weekend, or Cunningham will talk to everyone—the papers, ESPN, the DA."

"What'd you tell him?"

"I told him I'd give him an answer tomorrow."

"You didn't tell him no?"

"I wanted him to at least think I was takin' this seriously, so I said I'd think about it. I'm gonna tell him no tomorrow."

This didn't make any sense to Owen. These guys didn't care whether Nick was taking this seriously. All they cared about was whether he did it. Owen knew that the only reason Nick wouldn't have said no on the call today was that he was actually thinking about doing it. He started to give Nick a pep talk, trying to bolster his resolve. Nick cut him off.

"I know, Owen. I'm not gonna do it. I'll tell him that tomorrow."

"Listen, Sully, when you tell him no, tell him that you're not worried about what Cunningham will say. You know, that no one'll believe Cunningham, that you still have a witness who'll back up your story. Maybe they'll realize they're overplaying their hand and back off."

"Yeah, right, Owen," Nick replied sarcastically. "I'm sure these are the kinda guys who'll just walk away."

Owen was quiet for a moment. "Did this guy give you his name, Nick?"

"No."

"How about a phone number?"

"He didn't give me a number—he said he'd call me back. I can see the number he called from on my phone, though."

"Why don't you give me the number. It's probably a disposable cell phone, but I'll see if I can find out anything about it."

Nick gave him the number and then said, "Alright, man, thanks for everything."

"You OK? You want me to come out there? I can probably take a few days off."

"Nah, I'll be OK. Don't worry about it. I'll call you tomorrow."

"This guy say what time he was gonna call?" asked Owen.

"No. But we fly out to Chicago around dinnertime tomorrow. If I don't hear from him by about three, I'm gonna call the number he called from today."

"OK, Sully, hang tough. Talk to you tomorrow."

Owen ended the call in an apprehensive mood. He was growing increasingly worried that Nick would give in to those threats and agree to throw the game. His last attempt to outmaneuver Cunningham—more accurately, outmaneuver whatever mobsters were pulling Cunningham's strings—had backfired in a tragic way. Now he knew he needed to come up with something else to keep Nick from making a big mistake. As he pondered his next move, he thought back to the name Cunningham had dropped during their confrontation at the St. Regis a few days ago.

After another minute of turning over various possibilities in his head, Owen called Jack Ludwick. He got voice mail and left a message asking Ludwick to call back as soon as possible on an urgent matter. Owen was packing up to leave the office at about seven thirty when Ludwick called back.

"Hey, Jack, thanks for calling back."

"How'd things work out with that Lombardo guy?" asked Ludwick. "Were you able to get in touch with him?"

The mention of Dante threw Owen off momentarily. He took a few seconds to regain his composure and then said, "Actually, things didn't work out very well at all with that. But you did your job—the information you got for me was just what I needed."

"So you have another job for me?"

"Yeah, two things. First, I'd like you to see if you can track down who a cell phone is registered to." He gave Ludwick the number.

"OK, this won't take long. That info's either available or it isn't. I'll tell you, though, with all the disposable cell phones they sell today, there's a good chance I come up empty on this."

"Understood. The second thing is, I want you to find out whatever you can for me about a guy. His last name's Spinelli—I don't have a first name. There's only two things I can tell you about this guy. One, he lives somewhere in the Boston area, maybe even southern New Hampshire. Two, he's a mob guy. I don't know who he works for. I know he's into gambling, maybe other stuff. Also, I think he's somewhat high up in whatever criminal organization exists around Boston these days—he probably runs a crew of guys."

"I know better than to ask you why you want that info, but that *is* an interesting request." Ludwick paused briefly. "Is that all you got on him?"

"That's it."

"You know, it's not like the mobsters around here have their own website, with an org chart of names and titles and stuff. Tracking down information on the mob isn't easy."

"C'mon, Jack, I know that's just a windup to telling me how much you want to charge me for this. I'll tell you what. I'm in the same hurry for this as I was for tracking down Dante Lombardo. I know it's a weekend, so I'll pay you what I did for you for that first job—double your normal rate. But I need you to get on this right away."

"OK, Owen, it's a deal. I'll check in with you tomorrow, or Sunday at the latest, let you know what I've come up with."

Chapter 31

Ron Del Blanco, the Red Wings trainer for the past twenty-one years, removed the ice pack from Nick's right calf and began gently stretching the muscle. It was just after one thirty on Saturday afternoon. Nick had been pushing hard during sprints at the end of practice when he felt a sharp pain in his calf. Showing heart but not necessarily good judgment, Nick completed the remaining sprints but found himself limping in pain after taking off his skates in the locker room following practice. Del Blanco quickly diagnosed it as a muscle strain and began the ice and stretching routine. Del Blanco had been an assistant trainer for the Detroit Tigers before joining the Red Wings. He knew this injury would keep a baseball player out of the lineup for a few weeks. He also knew that if this had happened to Nick—or most NHL players—in the middle of a game, there wasn't a chance in hell he would've even missed a shift.

Returning to his locker, Nick saw the missed call icon on his cell phone. A quick check revealed the call had come from the same number as had yesterday afternoon's call. Nick hurriedly dressed and walked gingerly out of the rink. As soon as he was in his car, before even starting the engine, Nick, his stomach in knots, returned the call.

A familiar voice exclaimed, "Nicky boy, what's shakin'?"

"Who's this?"

"You don't recognize my voice, Nicky? Should I be offended, or are you just a fuckin' moron?"

"I recognize your voice."

"Alright, now we're gettin' somewhere. You know why I'm callin', then. The moment of truth has arrived for you, my friend. So you gonna play ball with us? Or you gonna make me ruin your fuckin' life?"

Nick paused for what felt to him like an eternity but was actually less than ten seconds. He swallowed audibly. "I'll do it."

"Good boy, Nicky. Some of my associates had their doubts, but I knew you'd come through. You got too much to lose by fuckin' with us."

"So what now?" asked Nick.

"Whaddaya mean, 'What now'? It's pretty goddamn simple. You make sure you lose next Saturday. That's it, end of story."

"So I won't be hearing from you again?"

"As long as you lose, you won't hear from me again. But lemme tell you what happens if for some bizarre reason the Red Wings win. If you think Cunningham tells his story then, you got it all wrong. See, right now Nick, you don't go along with this, it's a missed opportunity for me. And fuckin' up your life seems like a good response for that. But now that you told me you're in, me and my boys are gonna be laying down some pretty heavy bets on this game. You don't come through now, we're out of a lot of fuckin' money. That happens, Nick, you won't hear from me again. *'Cause you'll never see it fuckin' comin'!* You win, and you'll be dead within a day."

* * *

Nick was sitting in his kitchen, rehearsing what he was going to say to Owen. His plan, insofar as he'd come up with one, was to tell Owen that he refused to throw the game, because he knew Owen wouldn't stop hounding him if Owen thought he was even thinking about throwing the game. What he'd tell Owen after next Saturday was something Nick hadn't worked out yet. Nick knew he'd be hearing from Owen shortly after three o'clock if he didn't call Owen before then. It was just before three when he finally placed his call to Owen.

"Sully, what's up?"

"Hey, Owen," he replied.

"You hear from the guy?"

"Yeah, he just called. I'll tell ya, man, this is gettin' old."

"How'd it go?"

"I told him I wasn't gonna do it."

Whereas Owen had expected an animated, combative Nick, his voice was flat. This worried Owen.

"What'd he say?"

"Same threats. Cunningham's going to the DA, ESPN, the Detroit beat writer."

"What'd you say?"

"I told him no one will believe Cunningham. That we still got a witness who'll back up my story."

Owen wasn't sure whether to believe Nick. Nick seemed to be parroting what Owen had told him the evening before rather than genuinely recounting a conversation he had just had.

"How'd he react to that?" Owen asked.

Nick paused. "He didn't really react to it. He just swore at me and said I'd be sorry for not doing what they wanted."

"No additional threats?"

"No. And I just hung up after that."

"Did he say when Cunningham was going to go public with his story?"

"No. But I'm thinking they'll wait until after the Bruins game."

"Why?"

"That'll still give 'em time to try to get me to throw the game."

Or, Owen thought, *that could be a convenient explanation for why Cunningham isn't telling the world about Nick even though Nick has supposedly told those guys no.* His doubts about whether Nick was being truthful with him were growing. He needed time to think.

"Nick, you gotta change your number right away."

"Yeah, I know. We get back from Chicago tomorrow night. I'll do it Monday morning."

"We also have to start thinking about our plan of attack for whenever Cunningham does start talking to people. You know, who we call first, who makes the call, that kinda stuff."

"Yeah, you're right," said Nick.

"You know what we oughta do, Sully. We should meet with your agent. He'll probably have some ideas on how to respond to this. I bet he has contacts at some good PR firms too. We should think about hiring someone like that."

The last thing Nick wanted to do was to tell his agent—or anyone—about this. In his mind, after next Saturday, he'd somehow move on from this, and no one would know what he'd done—either next Saturday in the Bruins game or ten years ago in Kingsbridge Park. As he searched for an excuse, Owen prompted him, "Sully, you still there?"

"Acutally, Owen, I think he's in Europe next week, checking out a couple of his European clients. You know, talking to them about whether they're ready to make the jump to the NHL."

"You must be able to get in touch with him, though—right?"

"Why don't we just wait till he's back. I think he's back next weekend."

"OK." Owen paused, feeling uneasy. "You know, Sully, no matter what happens, we're gonna figure out a way to deal with this. It'll work out."

"Thanks, Owen. I really mean that, man. Let's talk tomorrow."

Owen put down his phone and leaned back on his couch. He was absolutely sure Nick had agreed to throw the game.

Chapter 32

Sunday morning was as nice a morning as Boston had to offer for the beginning of February. The temperature was pushing fifty degrees, there wasn't a cloud in the sky, and the dusting of snow that had fallen the night before was still a glistening white on the Esplanade, the Back Bay park separating the bustle of Storrow Drive from the tranquility of the frozen Charles River. Owen was out for his usual Sunday-morning run. His route took him southwest through the Esplanade on the Boston side of the Charles, past local institutions such as Boston University and the giant Citgo sign overlooking Fenway Park. After crossing over the BU Bridge to the Cambridge side of the Charles, just blocks away from Harvard University, he ran along Memorial Drive, past MIT, before the Longfellow Bridge carried him back into Boston at the foot of Beacon Hill. On this particular Sunday morning, he was almost to the Longfellow, sweating profusely in the unseasonable temperature, when his cell phone rang.

Stopping to check the caller ID, he saw that it was Nick calling. He took a moment to catch his breath and then answered.

"Sully, what's up?"

"Hey Owen. Hey, I meant to ask you yesterday, do you know what the story is with Dante's funeral and stuff?"

"Yeah, I do, actually. I talked to his brother Peter yesterday. He's still in the army—he's down in San Antonio. He's coming up tomorrow night. Since he's not in the area, I volunteered to make the arrangements for the funeral and the wake. He even asked me to do the eulogy. The wake's Tuesday night, and the funeral is Wednesday morning. They're both up in Pennington."

"Jeez, you've gotta deal with that stuff on top of all the other shit goin' on?" exclaimed Nick.

"It's no big deal. Somebody's gotta do it."

"Is Dante's father in the area?"

"No, his brother told me he's down in South Carolina. His brother's been in touch with him. I guess he's coming up for the services."

"That's awfully big of him," said Nick sarcastically.

"Yeah, well, you remember what he was like."

"Sure do."

"How about you—are you going to be able to get out here?"

"I think so. We play here in Chicago this afternoon, then our next game isn't until Thursday night at home. So I should be able to fly in sometime Tuesday. What time's the wake?"

"It's five to seven Tuesday evening," said Owen. "At Fleury's. The funeral's ten o'clock Wednesday morning."

"Is the funeral at St. Xavier?"

"Yeah."

"I'm not sure if I'll be there for the wake, I gotta figure out what time we practice that day and check flight times. But I'll definitely be at the funeral on Wednesday."

"Are you flying into Boston or Manchester?"

"I don't know yet, I gotta figure all that out."

"Let me know once you know. I might be able to pick you up at the airport, depending on what time you get in."

"Thanks, man," said Nick.

"And call me right away if anyone calls you on that other situation."

"OK, will do. Talk to you soon."

* * *

After finally getting Nick to agree to throw the Bruins game, Spinelli spent parts of Saturday and Sunday attempting to set up a meeting with someone high up in the Salvaggio family. He had never actually met anyone from the family—in the current pecking order, Romero Matricula, the underboss for the greater Boston area, stood between Spinelli and the Salvaggios. But the guy who ran things in Worcester reported directly to the Salvaggio family, and Spinelli knew a couple of guys in the Worcester organization. A few phone calls by Spinelli yielded a number for Brian Jensen, one of the Salvaggio capos who kept a loose watch on things in New England for the family.

Spinelli was taking a chance, going behind Matricula's back. But Spinelli didn't lack for balls. And he felt reasonably sure that greed would trump any loyalty the Salvaggio organization might feel toward Matricula. After a couple of tries, Spinelli got through to Jensen midday on Sunday.

"Is this Brian Jensen?"

"Yeah, who's this?"

"My name's Vinnie Spinelli. I run a crew up here in the Boston area."

"You work for us?"

"Indirectly. I pay Matricula. So some of my earnings makes its way to you guys."

"So you work for Matricula. Whaddaya callin' me for?"

"I got a business proposition for ya."

"Why me?" asked Jensen.

"I got your name from a guy I know in Worcester. He said you were a player in the Salvaggio family. He also said you were smart."

"I'm listenin'."

"I think I got a way to fix an NHL game," said Spinelli. "We can both make a huge score bettin' on the game."

"So lemme ask you again. Why you comin' to me with this, not Matricula?"

Spinelli paused ever so briefly. He was about to push all his chips to the middle of the table. The road he was going down could accelerate his ascent within the

New England organized crime hierarchy. It could also get him killed.

"Matricula's a worthless piece of shit. He should be takin' a lot more money outa this area than he does. But he's too fuckin' lazy and stupid."

Jensen chuckled. "You got a set of balls on ya."

"Tell me I'm wrong," said Spinelli.

Jensen said nothing.

"Here's the deal. Fixin' a pro sports game's not an easy thing to pull off. This'll show you I can take care of business. I'll let you in on this so you and your guys can make some money. What I want in return is, I want you guys to let me take out Matricula."

Jensen let out a low whistle. "You're talkin' some serious shit here."

"I'm a serious guy."

"That may be true. But I don't know you from fuckin' Adam. For all I know, you're one of Matricula's guys tryin' to figure out whether we really got his back."

"You know Matricula doesn't have the brains to try something like that."

Jensen was silent for a moment. "Let me ask around about you. I'll get back to you—one way or the other."

Chapter 33

Late that Sunday evening, Owen sat at his kitchen table, with a legal pad and an empty cup of coffee in front of him and crumpled pieces of paper surrounding him. The Red Wings-Bruins game was only six days away, so his window of time to act was closing. He had spent the last two hours outlining and then refining his strategy. His plan was based in large part on a series of phone conversations he'd had that day with two individuals who had proven to be of great help to him.

The first of those persons was Jack Ludwick. Ludwick called him early that afternoon to report back on his latest assignment. Although he struck out on the cell-phone number Owen had asked about, he had significantly more luck in tracking down information on Vinnie Spinelli. As Owen furiously took notes, Ludwick relayed what he had come up with over the last two days—and it was a considerable amount.

Ludwick had started with online research, and although he was able learn a fair bit of basic information about Spinelli, not much of it was particularly interesting. From there Ludwick made two calls Friday night to friends in the Massachusetts State Police. Those calls produced no useful information about Spinelli, but the second guy he talked to had a good friend on the state police Organized Crime Task Force; he agreed to call his friend and ask him to speak with Ludwick. The friend called Ludwick back Saturday afternoon, and they spoke for about twenty minutes. As it turned out, the state cops viewed Spinelli as an up-and-comer in the world of organized crime and had been keeping tabs on him for the last six months. He provided Ludwick with all kinds of material on Spinelli, both facts and rumors.

Ludwick's last source of information was the brother of one of Ludwick's employees. This guy floated around the periphery of the Boston organized crime scene—Ludwick suspected he fenced stolen goods but wasn't sure—and had been a useful source of intelligence for Ludwick in the past. He was initially reluctant to talk with Ludwick about Spinelli; in his words, "It wouldn't be good for my health if Spinelli found out I was talking to you about him." After a little bit of prodding, and the promise of $1,000, the brother agreed to listen to what Ludwick had learned on his own and confirm it if he was able to. Ludwick was mildly surprised when the brother either confirmed everything he had heard from the state cop—even what the cop had categorized as speculation or rumor—or reported that he had heard the same rumor.

The picture of Spinelli that Ludwick painted for Owen was not welcome news to Owen. In short, Spinelli was smart, successful, ambitious, and violent. Though organized crime in New England had for years been infected with nepotism, Spinelli had ascended to his current perch on his own. To put his information in context, Ludwick had to spend a few minutes explaining to Owen the pecking order of New England organized crime and who the current players were. He then told him that although Spinelli had worked his way up the food chain to the point where he ran his own crew, he was far from content in his current position. According to Ludwick's source with the state police, there were whispers that Spinelli was angling for Matricula's position—underboss of the greater Boston area.

To Owen, Spinelli's scheme to fix the hockey game fit seamlessly into this mosaic. It required cunning and violence, and it offered not only a big financial score but also a chance to earn points with the guys controlling New England organized crime. Based on the information Ludwick gave him and Cunningham's offhand remark that Spinelli was trying impress some "New York big shots," Owen suspected Spinelli was bypassing Matricula and working with the New York family.

After thanking Ludwick and hanging up, Owen spent some time trying to figure out what Spinelli's plan looked like. His initial thought was that Spinelli was trying to demonstrate to the New York family, by arranging for the fixed game and letting them bet on it, that they should elevate him to underboss in replacement of Matricula. After thinking about it some more, though, he concluded that an equally plausible scenario was that Spinelli was letting the New York family in on the fix in exchange for permission to kill Matricula, thus paving the way for his ascension to underboss.

To clear his head, Owen took a midafternoon walk through Boston Common. In the nicer weather, the Common was a haven for skateboarders, street musicians, and beggars. But on this winter afternoon, Owen was pretty much alone with his thoughts and able to focus without interruption as he traversed the pathways lacing the Common. By the end of his walk, an idea had begun to germinate.

    Upon returning home, Owen called his father. Though Mark Anderson's legal practice was based in New Hampshire, he had good contacts throughout the New England legal community due to his active participation in regional bar associations. Explaining that one of his firm's clients had gotten caught up in a bribery investigation by the FBI, Owen asked his father for the name of a well-connected Boston criminal attorney. He told his father he needed someone with experience in RICO cases—RICO was the acronym for the Racketeer Influenced and Corrupt Organizations Act that was frequently used to target organized crime—so a lawyer who had represented mob figures would be preferable. He also didn't want any bottom-feeders—he wanted someone who was well regarded in that field. Mark said he had two possible names in mind but wanted to make some further inquiries about them. Owen impressed upon him the urgency of the situation, so Mark agreed to try to get back to Owen that evening.

    While waiting for a callback from his father, Owen placed another call to Ludwick late Sunday afternoon and asked him to track down two pieces of information for him—the name of Spinelli's attorney and the name of Romero Matricula's attorney. Ludwick told him he could probably find that out from his contacts with the state police, but it would have to wait until tomorrow. After Owen explained it was urgent and offered Ludwick a modest bonus, Ludwick agreed to make the calls that night.

It was just after seven o'clock when Mark Anderson got back to Owen. He had two names for him. Both had represented reputed mob guys on RICO charges in the last five years, and both had a reputation for being men of their word.

Owen needed one more piece of the puzzle to fall into place. About an hour later, Ludwick called back. He first informed Owen that Spinelli had been arrested twice in the last year. Both times the charges were dropped, but both times he employed the services of Ethan Wolf, an attorney from Cambridge. Nervously playing with his pen, Owen waited for the second, more crucial piece of information. Ludwick then reported that about six months ago, when Matricula was called before a grand jury in a gambling investigation run by the state cops, he had been represented by a Boston attorney named Joe Brogna.

Bingo! Brogna was one of the defense attorneys Mark Anderson had recommended. Owen smiled for the first time that day.

"Awesome, Jack, thanks. You earned that bonus. Now I got something else for you."

"Please just tell me it's not something you need tonight."

"No, I don't need anything else from you tonight. This is a job for tomorrow, maybe the next couple of days too. It doesn't even have to be you—one of your guys can handle this."

"Whaddaya got?" asked Ludwick.

"I want you to follow Vinnie Spinelli," said Owen. "I'm not interested in anything he does around here. I'm betting that he goes to New York City sometime in the next few days. If he does, I want your guy to follow him there and try to get some pictures of whoever he meets with down there."

"That's no problem if Spinelli drives down there. If he flies, my guy can get on the plane with him. But when they land there, he's probably gonna have to follow him by cab. And that may or may not work—then you're in the hands of the cabbie."

"If he does fly, just have your guy do the best he can. But I'm guessing he drives. That way there's no record of him going there."

"You're probably right. Plus it's cheaper. A lot of these mob guys are notorious tight asses. I'll have a guy outside his place when he wakes up tomorrow. I'll call you if he heads to New York."

Owen hung up with Ludwick and set to work outlining his plan. By ten o'clock that night, he was satisfied that he had something with at least a fifty-fifty chance of working.

Chapter 34

The Corona Diner was located in a hardscrabble section of Queens, and the diner's shabby decor was a perfect fit for the neighborhood. It was three o'clock on Monday afternoon and, as he had been instructed to do, Vinnie Spinelli sat alone in a booth in the back corner of the diner. The booths immediately to his left and right were empty, even though the diner was fairly busy. Spinelli suspected that was no coincidence.

Jensen had called Spinelli back on Monday morning. He didn't have much to say on the phone; he simply instructed Spinelli to meet him at this diner on Monday at three o'clock. Although Spinelli had been in the business long enough to know that anything could happen, he was feeling fairly confident. He figured that if the Salvaggios wanted to kill him, they'd either hit him up in the Boston area when he had his guard down or Jensen would've instructed him to come to a less public setting.

At 3:10 p.m. two men entered the diner and scanned the place. One of the men then left the diner and stood wait outside. The other walked over and slid into the booth opposite Spinelli. He sized up Spinelli for a moment and then asked, "Vinnie Spinelli?"

"That's right." Spinelli had reminded himself to be more respectful, less confrontational, than was his wont.

Jensen extended his hand. "Brian Jensen."

Spinelli shook it without saying a word. He figured waiting for Jensen to speak was the proper protocol.

"I did some checking up on you," Jensen continued.

After a few seconds of silence, Spinelli decided it would be rude not to respond. "You like what you hear?"

"I didn't, I wouldn't be meetin' with you."

Spinelli replied, "You didn't, I probably wouldn't be meetin' with anyone."

Jensen smiled for the first time. "You wanna know who we talked to?"

"Sure."

"We started with Matricula."

Spinelli said nothing, but a touch of alarm registered in his face.

"Relax. I told him we were just doing a routine check on all his bigger crews, seeing who was carryin' their weight and who wasn't."

"If he knew I was even thinkin' of comin' after him, I'd be dead within a day," said Spinelli.

"You're right about that. But don't worry, he's got no idea why we were askin'."

"Who else you talk to?"

"One guy in Worcester. And one guy who works for you." Jensen again read Spinelli's face as a look of anger flickered across it. "You shouldn't be surprised to hear that we got sources everywhere."

"So what did ya hear?"

"It sounds like you run a pretty good crew up there," said Jensen. "Not big, but effective. You think outside the box, do what needs to be done. And sometimes you step on toes, piss people off."

"In this business, you don't do that, you get eaten alive."

"I didn't say I thought it was a bad thing," said Jensen. "Some people might call how you operate aggressive, even treacherous. I call it enterprising."

It was Spinelli's turn to flash a brief smile. "Sounds like you and me are gonna get along."

"We'll see. Depends on if you deliver what you say you can deliver."

"I'll deliver. I already got my bets in."

"How much you got ridin' on this game?"

"About two hundred and fifty grand. I got it broken down into almost one hundred different bets with different bookies and online books so no one gets suspicious."

"Jesus, two hundred and fifty grand. You must be sure you got this thing sewn up."

"I got it covered. And once I pull this off? What we talked about with Matricula, you OK with that?"

Jensen looked at Spinelli silently for a moment. When he spoke, he spoke deliberately, choosing his words carefully. "We got no real beef with Matricula. He's sorta content sittin' on what he has, doesn't do much to grow the business. But he provides a pretty steady cash flow to us, and he polices his territory pretty good. So we'd have no problem leavin' him in place." He paused again. "But it would take some brains and some balls to do what you say you can do. You show us you can pull that off, my bosses think it'd be a good thing to let a guy like you have a bigger role in the organization. So yeah, we're OK with you takin' out Matricula. *If* you deliver."

Spinelli nodded. "I 'preciate that. I'll deliver."

"One other thing. You're on your own going after Matricula. You get it done, you got our blessin's. But it goes wrong, we don't know anything about it. You swing and miss, we wanna let business go on just the way it was."

"I unnerstan'. I wouldn't expect it to be any other way."

"You worried about gettin' to Matricula? He don't lack for muscle, ya know."

"No, I'm not worried. As long as he's got no idea it's comin', it won't be hard to get to him. He's careful, but his guard's not up all the time."

* * *

Owen's cell phone chirped just before three thirty on Monday afternoon. He had been meeting with a first-year associate, discussing a research assignment Owen had given her. But seeing the name on the caller ID, Owen informed her he had to take this call and promised to catch up with her later that day. After waiting a few seconds for her to leave his office, Owen answered the call.

"Hey, Sergio. What's up?"

Sergio was the guy Ludwick had watching Spinelli. Earlier that day Sergio had followed Spinelli onto the

Massachusetts Turnpike heading west, through the tony western suburbs of Boston and eventually past Worcester. Once Spinelli exited the Turnpike in Sturbridge onto Route 84 West—which almost certainly meant he was heading for New York City—Sergio had called Ludwick. Ludwick had conferenced in Owen, introducing him to Sergio, and Sergio had relayed to Owen what he had just told Ludwick. Owen had asked Sergio to check in with him periodically throughout the day. The first update had come when Spinelli arrived at the Corona Diner. This was the second.

"Spinelli left the diner about ten minutes ago. He just got on Two Ninety-Five North. Looks like he's headed back to Boston."

"So what happened at the diner? He meet someone there?"

"Yeah. About fifteen minutes after I called you, two guys showed up. Even as they were walking up to the diner, I was pretty sure they were the guys who'd be meeting with Spinelli. Just something about the way they carried themselves. They kinda gave off a 'don't fuck with me' vibe, ya know?"

"Did they meet with him inside the diner?" asked Owen.

"Yeah. They both went in and checked out the joint. Then the bigger of the two guys stood outside, like he was a bouncer or somethin'. Oh, and he was carryin' a gun. I recognized the little bulge in the small of his back. The other guy—the sharp dresser—went over and sat in

Spinelli's booth. They talked for about ten minutes. Then that guy left, and Spinelli left about two minutes later."

"How good a view did you have of them?"

"Pretty good. I was sittin' in my car in the parking lot, probably twenty-five feet away. The place is pretty much all windows. I could see the booth Spinelli and the other guy were sittin' in. Spinelli's back was to me, but I could see the other guy's face."

"Did you get any pictures?" asked Owen.

"Yeah, a few of Spinelli going into the diner. Then I got some of the two of 'em sittin' in the booth together, though you can't see Spinelli's face too good. And I got a picture of the two New York guys leavin', then Spinelli leavin'."

"Great. Could you get a sense of the tone of the meeting? I mean, did it seem friendly, were they arguing, that kind of thing?"

"It seemed friendly enough. I'd say it started off kinda businesslike. But the other guy smiled a few times. And at the end, they shook hands, and the other guy kinda patted Spinelli on the shoulder. Like they had some kinda deal or something."

"Great, Sergio, thanks. That's just what I needed to hear. If Spinelli makes any other stops, let me know. If he just comes back to Boston and heads home, you're all done; you can stop following him."

"Got it. So you'll only hear from me if he meets with anyone else."

"OK, thanks, Sergio."

After hanging up with Sergio, Owen made two other calls. First he scheduled an appointment for Tuesday afternoon with Joe Brogna. The second call was to Ethan Wolf's office; Owen set up a meeting with him on Wednesday afternoon.

Chapter 35

Dawn broke in southern New Hampshire on Wednesday morning, but not without a struggle. The area was shrouded in fog, and a cold drizzle fell as Owen and Nick drove together to Fleury's Funeral Home. Nick had flown into Manchester from Detroit the previous night. Owen had picked him up at the airport after leaving Dante's wake. Both men had stayed at their parents' houses in Pennington on Tuesday night. They arrived at Fleury's at 9:20 a.m., ten minutes before the procession was scheduled to depart the funeral home for St. Xavier Church.

There were only about ten people at Fleury's. In addition to Owen and Nick, Dante's father and brother were there, along with two of Dante's aunts and a few high school friends. At precisely nine thirty, the funeral director said a few words, and then the four pallbearers—Owen, Nick, Mr. Lombardo, and Peter Lombardo—placed the casket into the hearse. The four of them rode in silence to St. Xavier, trailed by a minicaravan of five cars.

As he helped carry the casket into St. Xavier, Owen was pleased to see there was a decent-sized crowd there, perhaps seventy-five people—although even that looked somewhat sparse in the spacious cathedral. Cunningham was seated near the back of the church. When Owen spotted him, his feelings of bitterness were mixed with relief that Cunningham had shown up. As he walked closer to the front of the church, Owen nodded to his parents, who were seated in a pew to his left.

The four pallbearers sat in the front row, to the right of the center aisle. Seated by herself on the left side of the front row was a young woman holding a toddler. Owen assumed that was Dante's wife and daughter.

Father Powers, the longtime principal of St. Xavier High School, said the funeral mass. Owen paid little attention to the service; he was too busy rehearsing the eulogy in his head. He had spent a lot of time crafting the words he'd soon be uttering, and he wanted to remember the eulogy exactly as he'd written it. After the communion service was completed, Father Powers called Owen to the altar.

Taking his place at the lectern, Owen scanned the congregation, confirming that Cunningham was still there. He then briefly bowed his head before proceeding.

"On behalf of Dante's family and friends, I want to thank you all for coming today. Mourning the passing of anyone is difficult. Mourning the passing of someone who was taken from us at such a young age is even harder. I'm sure we all wish we didn't have to be in this church today. But try to take some comfort in the fact that your presence here honors Dante, his life and his memory.

"My message to you today is really a simple one: Dante was a good man. Dante wasn't perfect—none of us are—and life presented Dante with more than his fair share of difficulties to deal with. But the true measure of a man is how much you do for others. And we should all strive to be half the man that Dante was in that regard.

"Dante and I have known each other since kindergarten. I've been fortunate enough to make a number of friends growing up in Pennington, during college, and in my brief career. But I can tell you in all honesty that I've never had a friend who was more loyal or more dependable than Dante. He was always there for a friend, no matter what the circumstances. If you really think about it, that's a pretty rare trait in today's world.

"Dante also exhibited an uncommon respect for others. He was very popular in high school, but he was never one of those kids who looked down on or taunted those who might have been on the outside of his social circle. And while I wouldn't presume to speak for them, I feel certain that Father Powers here, or any of the other teachers at St. Xavier, would tell you that Dante was one of the more respectful, courteous kids to walk the halls of that school.

"Another testament to the type of person Dante was is his military service. He spent four years in the mountains of Afghanistan, sleeping in caves, eating bugs, and risking his life every day. He didn't do that for money, or fun, or career advancement. He did it because he wanted to serve his country. How many of us would be willing to do that?

"I assume that, if you're here today, you all knew Dante to some degree. So what I've told you about him so far is probably not news to you. But what I'm about to tell you is something that none of you know.

"I suspect most of you are aware that ten years ago, Dante served about a year in jail for accidentally killing a man in a fight in Kingsbridge Park. Well, I'm here to tell you this morning what should have been said a long time ago: Dante did not kill that man."

There were several audible gasps in the congregation. Owen noticed Dante's father staring intently at him. Seated immediately to his left, Nick had a look of confusion on his face. Owen continued.

"What happened that night was a horrible accident. There was a fight on the beach—a fight started by the man who was eventually killed. Two young men—boys, really—from Pennington defended themselves against two members of a motorcycle gang. Driven by adrenaline and fear, one of those boys—not Dante—grabbed a chain from a biker and swung it at him. Although the intent was self-defense rather than aggression, the chain caught the man in the neck, cutting his jugular vein and causing the man to bleed to death.

"In the aftermath of the fight, Dante told the police that he was the one who swung the chain and accidentally killed the man. That wasn't true, but he said it to protect a friend. Because that's the kind of person Dante was—someone who would do anything for a friend." Owen paused and briefly made eye contact with Nick, noting that his earlier expression of confusion had turned to alarm. Looking back out over the congregation, Owen said, "That friend was me. I'm the one who killed that man."

A low murmur swept through the church. Before continuing, Owen quickly checked the reactions of his parents, who looked like they were in shock. He would have to catch up with them later to assure them that everything would work out all right. He also glanced at Nick, who now looked pissed off.

"I was injured slightly in the fight and was taken to the hospital. It was while I was in the hospital that Dante talked to the police and claimed to be the person responsible for the man's death. When I later found out what he had done, I tried to talk him out of it, but he refused to change his story. In hindsight, I didn't try hard enough. While Dante was always the paragon of a good friend, I failed him as a friend back then. Just like I failed him as a friend by losing touch with him over the last several years, and not being there for him when he went through some difficult times.

"Although I am sorry for not being the friend I should have been, I can act like a friend to him now. The one last thing I can do for him is clear his name, and let you all know he wasn't responsible for that tragedy in Kingsbridge Park. I hope and pray that what I've said here today will help you all see Dante for the outstanding person that he truly was, and that you will carry with you nothing but good memories of him. Thank you."

Chapter 36

Nick was pissed. For ten years he had carried with him the burden of knowing that Dante had sacrificed over a year of his life, and a part of his reputation, to protect him. Owen's eulogy perfectly echoed Nick's feelings of guilt over that. Now, Nick thought, he was going to have to live with whatever self-inflicted damage to Owen's life resulted from yet another false confession to Nick's crime. His mind raced as he thought about the possible ramifications to Owen. Could he go to prison for this? Would he lose his job? Would Owen's friends and family think he was noble for "admitting" what he did or cowardly for concealing it all these years? He glared at Owen as he and the other pallbearers carried Dante's casket out of the church.

After loading the casket into the hearse, Nick took Owen by the elbow and steered him about twenty feet away from the group of people gathering outside the front entrance to St. Xavier Church.

"What the hell was that all about?" he asked, the frustration evident in his voice.

"Listen, we can talk in a minute, but right now I have to find Cunningham, before he takes off." Owen walked hurriedly toward the parking lot in back of the church. He saw Cunningham approaching his car, his back to Owen. "Ryan, hold up," Owen yelled, breaking into a jog.

Cunningham opened the door of his Corolla and started to get in. He then thought better of it and stood and leaned over the open door, facing Owen, who had stopped just in front of the car.

"You really are full of surprises, Anderson. First you track down Dante and trot him out. Then you tell everyone it was you that killed that biker. Your first move didn't work out so good. What're you tryin' to do with this one?"

For an instant the anger welled up in Owen, and he felt an urge to punch Cunningham. But, realizing the importance of sticking to his plan, he quickly suppressed it.

"Listen, Ryan, you need to get it through your head that your twisted little plan is over. We're back to where we were before your scumbag friends killed Dante. Nick's not throwing the game. And you've got no leverage to make him do it."

"I can still tell the world that Sully killed that biker," said Cunningham. "I know he doesn't want me to do that."

"You're not going to do that, Ryan, because you know no one will believe you. My word'll beat yours. Remember, you weren't even there. And I can prove I was—my injuries, plus I had blood from one of the bikers on my clothes. So doing that would be pointless. Just give it up."

Cunningham was silent. Owen detected a sense of resignation in his expression and body language. After a moment Cunningham said softly, "They're gonna kill me, man."

"I don't know why I even care what happens to you, after all the damage your fucked-up scheme has caused. But if I were you, I'd get outa the area. Go south, go west, go somewhere. Try to start a new life. But get away from the guys you owe money to. And get away from Nick and me."

Cunningham looked at Owen for what felt to him like a long time. He actually contemplated apologizing, but he knew that, minutes before Dante would be buried, it would ring hollow. So he simply nodded and said, "I will."

With that, Owen turned away from Cunningham and walked back toward the front entrance of the church, where Nick was making small talk with some old high-school friends. Owen felt the eyes upon him as he approached, and the conversation drifted to a halt when he joined the small group Nick was talking with. After an awkward moment, Owen said, "Sully, OK if I talk with you for a minute?" Nick nodded, and they excused themselves and walked a short distance away from the crowd.

"So you wanna tell me what's going on?" asked Nick, still agitated.

"Sully, you can't throw the game on Saturday. You've got too much to lose. I told you I'd help you get out of this mess. That's what I'm doing."

"I told you over the weekend that I told those guys I wasn't gonna do it."

"Nick, we've known each other long enough for me to be able to tell when you're bullshitting me. Look me in the eye and tell me you told them no."

Nick looked at Owen and started to speak, but he averted his eyes before he said anything. He then looked back at Owen, clearly embarrassed. "Owen, you know what they were threatening to do? Not just to me, but to you too?"

"Sully, you don't have to explain yourself to me. I probably would've done the same thing if I was in your shoes. So just forget about that. The only thing we have to focus on now is getting this mob guy to back down."

"So that's why you said it was you who killed that biker? You think that if Cunningham knows there's still someone around to say it wasn't me, maybe he won't go public with his story?"

"That's part of it. We needed something to convince Cunningham there's no point in telling his story. But it was also the right thing to do for Dante." Nick nodded silently. Owen continued. "I think we've still got a problem though, Sully. Even if Cunningham never says a word about what happened that night—and I don't think he will; I'll bet we don't hear from him again—I think this mob guy's not going to back off."

"I think you're right, Owen. This guy I talked to on Saturday said if the Red Wings beat the Bruins, he'd kill me."

"Yeah, I'm not surprised, Sully. I'm pretty sure I know who that guy is. He's an up-and-coming mob guy named Vincent Spinelli. From what I've been able to find out, he's smart, he's ruthless, and he's trying to convince the New York mob to let him have his boss's job—running things in the Boston area. I think fixing the game on Saturday is his way of showing the New York guys he's up for that."

"How the hell do you know all that?" asked Nick.

"Through a private detective I hired."

"You're shittin' me."

"Anyway, Spinelli went to New York on Monday and met with a New York mob guy. If you talked to Spinelli on Saturday, then I'm pretty sure he's already told the New York guys that he's got things lined up for the Bruins game this Saturday. And my guess is that Spinelli and the New York guys have already put down some heavy bets on the Bruins. So even without Cunningham, I don't think Spinelli is just gonna walk away from this."

"So where does that leave us?" asked Nick.

"I got a plan."

"You gonna tell me what it is?"

"Not until I know if it works," said Owen.

"Owen, this guy's threatening to kill me. He may come after you too. Maybe we should go to the cops."

"I thought about that, Sully. But we have no proof the guy who threatened you is Spinelli. It could've been anyone."

"But you're sure it's Spinelli?" asked Nick.

"Pretty damn sure, yeah," said Owen. "Cunningham let it slip that it was a guy named Spinelli who told him to blackmail you. And everything I've been able to find out about Spinelli—including his meeting in New York on Monday—points to him being the guy behind this. But that's not enough for the cops to do anything. Besides, once we start telling the story to the cops, we have to come clean about everything, including Cunningham's attempt to blackmail you. So I don't see how we avoid telling them what really happened in Kingsbridge Park. It might even come out that you told Spinelli you would throw the game."

Nick was silent for a moment. "I don't know, Owen. Going to the cops might still be our best move. Especially since I don't even know what your plan is."

"Nick, you've got to give me a day. I should know by tomorrow if it's going to work. If it doesn't look like it will, I'll fly out to Detroit tomorrow night and we'll regroup. We can talk then about to going to the cops."

Nick smiled wanly. "Alright, man. You know I've always said I'd trust you with my life. I think that's exactly what I'm doing now."

Owen nodded. "You're flying back to Detroit tonight, right?"

"Yeah, I've got a five-fifteen flight out of Manchester."

Owen clapped him on the shoulder. "If I know anything for sure, I'll call you tonight. But it'll probably be tomorrow before I get back to you." Owen glanced to his left, where Dante's father and brother were getting into the hearse. "Listen, we've got to head to the cemetery.

Try to put this whole mess out of your head for a while. We'll know a lot more by tomorrow."

* * *

Cunningham wasn't quite panicking, but he was close to it. Now that it looked like Nick wasn't going to go along with the plan after all, he genuinely feared for his life. He decided to follow Owen's advice and leave town. He wasn't sure exactly where he was going, but heading south seemed like a good idea, especially in February. After making two stops in Manchester—his bank, where he cleaned out his account (all $119.73), and a Sunoco station, where he used almost half of that money to fill his tank—he aimed his Corolla toward Route 93 south. For a moment he thought about calling Spinelli to tell him Nick wouldn't be throwing the game after all. He figured that could save Spinelli a lot of money, since he would still have time to call off his bets. But after thinking for a minute about what Spinelli had put him through, he said to himself, "Fuck Spinelli" as he accelerated up the highway entrance ramp.

Chapter 37

It was just before noon on Wednesday when Owen and Nick left the cemetery. They rode mostly in silence back to Nick's parents' house, where Owen dropped him off. After a quick stop for a sandwich in Pennington center, Owen headed south toward Boston. His appointment with Ethan Wolf—who counted Vincent Spinelli among his clients—was at two o'clock.

Wolf's office was on Brattle Street in Cambridge, one of the more prestigious locations greater Boston had to offer. It was situated in a modern three-story building near the crossover point between the fashionable shops and restaurants closer to Harvard Square and the million-dollar homes that dotted the treelined stretch of Brattle Street northwest of the Square.

After arriving at 1:50 p.m., Owen waited in a tastefully decorated reception area for Wolf's prior appointment to end. At about 2:10 p.m. two well-dressed, middle-aged men exited the office. Thirty seconds later a fiftyish man with close-cropped dark hair, graying at the sides, emerged. He was strong looking—thick but not fat—and wore dark-blue suit pants, a white shirt, and a bright-red tie with matching red suspenders. Quickly appraising Owen, he stuck out his hand.

"You must be Owen Anderson. Ethan Wolf."

Owen took a seat in a mahogany captain's chair, facing the massive desk that Wolf sat behind. Wolf engaged in just enough useless banter to avoid appearing rude before cutting to the chase.

"So, Owen, what brings you here today? You were a little vague with my assistant when you scheduled this appointment."

"I apologize, Mr. Wolf—"

"Call me Ethan, please," Wolf interrupted.

"You're a well-known attorney with an excellent reputation. I feel it'd be more respectful to call you Mr. Wolf, if you don't mind."

Impressed, Wolf nodded. Owen continued. "Again, I apologize for that. I wanted to keep the subject matter of our meeting between you and me. For now."

"Well, that's rather mysterious. May I assume you're ready to unburden yourself at this time?"

"I am. I have a story to tell you that involves one of your clients. A man named Vincent Spinelli."

Owen paused briefly, waiting for any reaction from Wolf. Wolf simply extended an open hand, indicating that Owen should proceed.

In as much detail as he could muster, hoping it would bolster his credibility, Owen recounted his tale. He started with what he knew about Spinelli—which was gleaned primarily from Jack Ludwick's research—including the designs he had on Romero Matricula's position. He then introduced Ryan Cunningham to the picture, telling of his considerable gambling debt to Spinelli's crew (Owen knew nothing about Cunningham's botched attempt to courier drugs for them) and explaining that Spinelli forced

Cunningham to leverage his relationship with NHL star Nick Sullivan to entice Sullivan to throw the game against the Bruins this coming Saturday. Fudging the truth for the first time in his story, Owen recounted how Cunningham threatened to falsely implicate Nick in the death of biker during a fight ten years ago if he didn't go along with Spinelli's scheme.

Wolf sat impassively, listening intently but asking no questions as Owen continued. Owen next described their countermove—finding the person responsible for the biker's death (Dante Lombardo) and telling Cunningham that his threat wouldn't work because the person who confessed to, and did time for, the killing would refute his story and no one would believe it. He then recounted the murder of Dante, implying without directly stating that Spinelli was behind it. It was there that Wolf interjected for the first time.

"Do you have anything at all that connects Mr. Spinelli to this unfortunate death?" he asked.

"Beyond what's implied by the circumstances and timing of his killing, no. But, as you'll see in a few minutes, tying Mr. Spinelli to that killing is not an important part of this story."

Wolf nodded. "Continue, please."

Owen went on to describe Spinelli's calls to Nick over the past weekend, following Dante's murder, during which Spinelli made various threats in an attempt to get him to throw the game. Nick acquiesced, Owen said, but he was just buying time and never intended to go through with it.

The next part of Owen's story was his admission, at Dante's funeral, that he was the one who had accidentally killed the man during the fight in Kingsbridge Park. He did that, he explained, to convince Cunningham not to go public with the claim that Nick was the person responsible. Owen told Wolf that he was fairly certain that had worked and that Cunningham was leaving town.

Wolf, with a small smile, asked Owen, "And was it really you who killed that man?"

"That also is irrelevant to the point of this story."

Wolf was still smiling, but his voice had an edge to it. "I must say, Mr. Anderson, this is quite an entertaining story. But if there is a point to it, I trust you will make your way to the vicinity of it soon."

"I'm within striking distance, Mr. Wolf."

Owen then told Wolf that he was reasonably certain Spinelli was not going to give up on his plan to fix the Red Wings-Bruins game on Saturday, with or without Cunningham's help, because he had too much riding on it. Relying on the information supplied by Ludwick's associate, Sergio, he described Spinelli's trip to New York on Monday. He even gave Wolf copies of a few of the pictures Sergio had taken of Spinelli's meeting with two "associates" from New York. Wolf was both surprised and impressed by the details Owen was able to provide about Spinelli's meeting with the New York mobster. Not wanting to concede that to Owen, however, he tried pressing him a bit.

"Do you even know the identity of the gentleman meeting with Mr. Spinelli?" he asked.

"No. But I'm willing to bet that Mr. Matricula would recognize him." When Wolf did not respond, Owen continued, "I don't know exactly what was said at that meeting. But would you like to hear my educated speculation?"

"Why not?"

"We both know Spinelli's got no use for Matricula. He wants his job—underboss of the greater Boston area. If he's going behind Matricula's back to meet with guys from the New York mob, that means he's trying to enlist their support for him to take over for Matricula. A pretty good way for him to earn his stripes with the New York guys would be to show them he can arrange to fix a pro hockey game—that's not an easy thing to pull off—and let the New York guys make some money betting on it. I don't know whether Spinelli is asking New York to elevate him to underboss, replacing Matricula, or asking them for permission to kill Matricula and just seize the position. But I'm pretty sure it's one or the other."

Wolf said nothing.

"So I've finally arrived at the punch line. I want to let you know that Nick Sullivan is not going to do anything to help the Bruins win the game Saturday. He'll be playing his heart out to win, like he always does. I'd appreciate it if you would convey that message to Mr. Spinelli. I also ask that you pass along two requests to Mr. Spinelli."

"I'm still a little confused here." Wolf was still cordial, but his tone had turned frosty. "You now *want* something from Mr. Spinelli?"

"We sure do."

"Am I correct in assuming that you're not asking me to represent you with respect to your requests of Mr. Spinelli? Because I'm afraid that would represent a conflict of interest on my part, given that Mr. Spinelli is already a client of mine."

"No, Mr. Wolf, I already have a lawyer. These are my requests. The first is that Mr. Spinelli have no further contact—either directly or through his associates—with Nick Sullivan, Ryan Cunningham, or myself. Second, we'd like Mr. Spinelli to establish a trust fund, for the benefit of Dante Lombardo's young daughter, in the amount of seven hundred and fifty thousand dollars. By the way, that amount was not chosen randomly. I suspect Mr. Spinelli's crew takes in more than a million a year. But I want this taken care of quickly, so we'll settle for what I bet he can get his hands on right away." Owen handed Wolf a piece of paper. "Here are the wire instructions for the trust account I've set up."

"Have you taken leave of your senses, Mr. Anderson?" Wolf asked with a humorless smile. "You've spun an interesting yarn here, which may or may not be true." He then leaned forward, his smile having evaporated. "But what makes you think that puts you in a position to make demands of a man like Mr. Spinelli?"

Owen remained composed. "I mentioned a moment ago that I have legal representation. Yesterday I met with an attorney named Joe Brogna. I retained Mr. Brogna for a possible civil suit against Mr. Spinelli in connection with the murder of Dante Lombardo and the blackmailing of Nick Sullivan. And I told him the same story I just told you, though I may have included an additional detail or two."

Wolf's smile now returned, as he seemed genuinely amused by Owen's audacity. "So I suppose I should take your demands as a settlement offer. Well, Mr. Anderson, since you don't appear to have any way to even come close to proving the allegations in your story, I must tell you that there's not the slightest chance Mr. Spinelli would ever accede to those demands."

"I wouldn't look at those requests as a settlement offer, Mr. Wolf. I don't think it's the threat of civil litigation that should cause Mr. Spinelli to agree to my requests."

"Oh, let me guess. Please, tell me if I'm close." Wolf leaned forward again. "If Mr. Spinelli doesn't comply with your requests, you or Mr. Brogna will go *straight* to the police with this information. And, if I may be even more dramatic, due to your unfounded view of Mr. Spinelli as a violent person, you instructed Mr. Brogna to bring this information to the police himself if any harm were to befall you." Wolf chuckled. "I must tell you, though, that as fascinating as your story may be, your utter lack of evidence to support it leaves me completely unconcerned with the threat of divulging it to the authorities." Wolf sat back in his chair with a self-satisfied smile.

"I'd say you're in the ballpark, Mr. Wolf, but you're wrong on some important details." He paused to gage Wolf's reaction, but Wolf's expression betrayed nothing. Owen continued. "I assume, given your contacts in the criminal-defense community, that you know that Mr. Brogna also represents Romero Matricula."

Wolf nodded silently, wondering where this was heading.

"And, being a lawyer, you know far better than I do what the attorney-client privilege is." The attorney-client privilege prohibits a lawyer from disclosing to any other person—without the client's consent—information that the lawyer obtained from the client relating to the matter the lawyer was hired for.

Wolf said nothing. Owen then extracted a piece of paper from a folder he was carrying and handed it to Wolf. "This is a copy of a letter I left with Mr. Brogna yesterday. It waives the attorney-client privilege, and allows Mr. Brogna to share my story with anyone he pleases, if the trust for Mr. Lombardo's daughter is not put into place by the end of the day tomorrow. The privilege is also waived if Nick Sullivan or myself is harmed in any way."

Owen waited a moment to let this sink in. Wolf tried to remain stoic, but Owen noticed some color creep into his face.

"If Mr. Brogna became free to pass this information along," Owen continued, "who do you think his first call would be to?"

In a small voice, Wolf responded, "I suppose it might be to Mr. Matricula."

"As a matter of fact, Mr. Brogna happened to mention to me that that's exactly who he'd call first if the privilege were waived."

Wolf remained silent. Owen continued. "Mr. Wolf, the point you made a few minutes ago about the police is correct. I probably don't have enough evidence to get the police to even investigate Mr. Spinelli, much less convict him of anything. But I think it's fair to say that Mr. Matricula would impose a far less strict evidentiary standard than our courts of law do. I'd be willing to bet that my story about Spinelli's plan—supported by the details and circumstantial evidence I do have—would be enough to spur action on the part of Mr. Matricula. Decisive action."

Owen waited for Wolf to speak. After a moment, Wolf said, "You've certainly got a set of stones on you."

"Listen, Mr. Wolf. It's not like I randomly decided to mess with Vincent Spinelli. I never even heard of him until a week ago. But he had one of my friends killed, and he threatened the life of another one. I'm just trying to look out for my friends."

"I need to confer with my client on this."

"I understand. But tomorrow's deadline stands."

"You'll hear from me tomorrow," said Wolf. "One way or the other."

As Owen walked out of Wolf's office, he wondered whether he should take that as a threat.

Chapter 38

Spinelli arrived at Wolf's office at nine thirty on Thursday morning, agitated. When Wolf had called him late the previous afternoon, Wolf had insisted on meeting with him first thing in the morning on an "urgent" matter but refused to tell him over the phone what it was. In Spinelli's mind, *he* set up meetings with Wolf, not the other way around. Spinelli was not a man who liked being told what to do. His mood would only get worse.

Wolf recounted his meeting with Owen the previous afternoon, describing Owen's demands and his threat. Spinelli was incensed.

"Who the fuck does that little cocksucker think he is? I'll show him what happens to guys who fuck with me!"

"Vincent, as distasteful as you may find it, his threat is a credible and formidable one."

"So what you're saying, in plain English, is you think this guy's got me by the balls?"

"It would seem so. I think we can both surmise what Romero Matricula would do if Anderson's information were passed on to him."

"Fuck that old man. I'll hit him before he hits me. Then I'll take care of Anderson and Sullivan too."

"Vincent, think this through. May I assume that Anderson's story is essentially accurate?"

Spinelli shrugged. "Pretty much."

"Then New York may have supported an insurrection against Matricula if you had delivered on the hockey game. But, were I in your shoes, I'd be extremely leery about moving against Matricula now that Sullivan is refusing to throw the game."

Spinelli abruptly rose from his chair and stalked angrily around the office. "Are you saying I should give in to this motherfucker? Leave him alone *and* pay him off?"

"Yes. That is a less than ideal outcome, but every alternative to that is worse for you."

Wolf and Spinelli argued for a few more miuntes—Spinelli enraged and Wolf composed—before Wolf was able to convince Spinelli to go along with Owen's request.

"Fuck me!" Spinelli exclaimed. "Alright, alright, I'll pay the fucker off."

"I think that's a wise decision, Vincent."

"Fuck you!"

Used to Spinelli's outbursts, Wolf continued calmly, "Vincent, can you access seven hundred and fifty thousand dollars?"

"Lemme think. I got over four hundred grand in stocks and bonds and shit with that financial guy you hooked me up with. Can I turn that into cash right away?"

"Probably. I'll call him when we're finished here to confirm that."

"I think I got a little over a hundred grand in my bank account. Plus I got a shitload of cash in a safe-deposit box and a safe in my basement. At least three hundred grand."

"We're going to have to get that cash into a bank account so it can be wired into the trust account Anderson has set up."

"Wait—don't they have rules against you depositing a bunch of cash into a bank account?" asked Spinelli.

"There are no rules that prohibit large cash deposits," said Wolf. "But for any deposit in excess of ten thousand dollars, the bank has to file a currency transaction report with the Treasury Department."

"What the fuck does that mean? Am I going to have feds snooping around, asking me where that money came from?"

"It's quite possible. Your most plausible story would probably be to claim that you won the money over the last month or so playing blackjack or poker at Foxwoods. I suggest you line up a few individuals who would be willing to testify that they witnessed your string of luck at that casino's card tables."

"Alright, I can do that."

"You're still officially an employee of that bar in Revere, correct?"

"Yeah. They give me a W-2 and everything, even though I never worked a day there."

"Good. So you can demonstrate a legitimate source of income. And you at least have a story to tell about your sudden influx of cash. You should be alright."

"But this means I'll have to pay fuckin' taxes on the cash I deposit, right?"

"Welcome to the real world, Vincent."

* * *

In all but the most inclement weather, Owen walked to and from work. On Thursday morning, however, uncertain of how Spinelli would respond to his demands and mindful of what had happened to Dante, Owen called a cab. When it arrived, he scanned Grove Street from his window—not really sure what he was looking for but figuring caution was in order—before hustling into the cab.

He spent a distracted and unproductive morning in his office, his eyes passing over the words in a report but not absorbing them. At 10:15 a.m. he took a break and called Sergeant Patterson from Saugus to ask about the investigation into Dante's murder.

Before making the call, Owen thought about whether he should reveal to Patterson his strong belief that Spinelli was behind the killing. He decided against it for two reasons. First, he was hoping he'd be able to cut his deal with Spinelli. If Spinelli later learned that Owen had pointed the murder investigation in his direction—which could well happen, given that Owen's account of Spinelli's attempt to blackmail Nick would provide a credible motive for the murder—Owen worried that Spinelli would not stick to his promise to leave Nick, Cunningham, and Owen alone. Second, he suspected Spinelli was smart enough to have used other people for the killing and to have an alibi in place for himself, so even if the cops looked at him, they probably would find nothing incriminating.

Owen was able to reach Patterson with his first call. "Hi, Sergeant Patterson, this is Owen Anderson calling. I'm checking in to see how your investigation into Dante Lombardo's killing is going."

Patterson was his usual brusque self. "If you're wondering whether we consider you a suspect, Mr. Anderson, the answer is no. We were able to verify your whereabouts during the timeframe when Mr. Lombardo was killed."

"That's a relief, I guess. Though I never thought you would look at me as a suspect."

"Everyone's a suspect until we rule them out, Mr. Anderson."

"Do you have any idea who did it?" asked Owen.

"No."

"Any real leads?"

"Not really," said Patterson.

There was a moment of awkward silence. "Sergeant Patterson, I don't know what protocol is in a situation like this. I'm not asking you to tell me anything that would jeopardize your investigation. But Dante was my friend. I just want to know if you think you're going to be able to find his killer."

Patterson sighed heavily. "Alright, Mr. Anderson, here's what I can tell you. We weren't able to recover any fingerprints or other forensic evidence from Mr.

Lombardo's body or from the site where we found his body. We also found nothing useful at your apartment, the last place he was known to be. We interviewed as many of your neighbors as we could. The only thing of note we heard was that a woman who lives in your building saw an unfamiliar black Ford Explorer parked on your street for quite a while on Friday, the day Lombardo was killed. But she didn't get a plate number or see anyone inside of it. Mr. Anderson, did you notice a black Ford Explorer in your neighborhood last week?"

Owen paused for a moment, thinking about whether he'd seen such a car in the area. "No, not that I remember."

"Well, I'm afraid we don't have much to go on here."

"So what you're saying is you have no leads, no suspects. That you're basically at a dead end?"

"We never give up on a murder investigation, Mr. Anderson. But I'll admit it looks far from promising right now."

After hanging up with Patterson, Owen halfheartedly got back to work, waiting for his cell phone to ring. At 11:13 a.m., it finally did.

Not recognizing the number, Owen nervously said, "Hello?"

"It's Ethan Wolf."

"Hello, Mr. Wolf."

"I met with Mr. Spinelli this morning. We had quite an interesting conversation."

Owen said nothing, waiting for him to continue. He was so tense that he had stopped breathing.

"Mr. Spinelli will agree to your demands, Mr. Anderson. I must tell you that it was not his initial inclination. But he eventually came to his senses. There is one twist, however. He will need an extra day to assemble the seven hundred and fifty thousand. Surely you can appreciate that marshaling funds of that amount involves liquidating some investments and moving assets around. We can wire the funds tomorrow. But not today."

This did not surprise Owen, and he had thought about how he would handle a request for more time. "I'll tell you what I can live with, Mr. Wolf. I can buy the fact that not all of the money is readily available. But I'm sure some of it is. As a show of good faith, I want at least two hundred and fifty thousand wired to the trust account today. If that happens today, I can wait until tomorrow for the rest of the money."

"I believe we'll be able to accommodate you with respect to the cash transfer," said Wolf. "Two hundred and fifty thousand will be wired today, and the rest will be sent tomorrow."

"Thank you."

"In addition to the trust-fund money, you also demanded that you, Mr. Sullivan, and Mr. Cunningham would not be, shall we say, interfered with by Mr. Spinelli. Are you looking for something in particular to provide you with assurances that will be the case?"

"No, Mr. Wolf. I think the receipt of the money gives me the comfort I need. If Spinelli were planning to come after us, there'd be no point in paying the money. Besides, what else could I get—a call from Spinelli promising to leave us alone? I think you can understand why his word wouldn't mean a whole lot to me."

"Very well, Mr. Anderson. A wire transfer of two hundred and fifty thousand will be made to the trust fund this afternoon. If you would be so kind as to call me to confirm receipt of it, I would appreciate that."

"I'll do that, Mr. Wolf," said Owen. "And I'll do the same tomorrow when the rest of it arrives."

"Good day, Mr. Anderson."

After talking with Wolf, Owen thought about calling Nick, but he resisted that urge. He wanted the first wire to hit, so he was sure Spinelli had accepted his terms, before he told Nick what was going on.

Owen had online access to the trust account he had set up for Dante's daughter, and he checked it continually over the next few hours to see if the money had hit. Nick called him around one o'clock, but Owen let it go through to voice mail. Finally, just before two thirty, a $250,000 wire transfer was posted to the trust account. Owen first made a quick call to Wolf to let him know the money had hit, and then he called Nick. He reached Nick in his car on his way home from the team's practice facility, where he had gotten some treatment on the calf muscle he had strained the previous weekend.

"Hey, man, I've been wondering when I'd hear from you," said Nick. "What's going on?"

"Sully, I think things are going to work out. I think we're going to be fine."

"So you gonna finally tell me what the hell's goin' on?"

Owen briefly described meeting with Joe Brogna on Tuesday and then recounted in detail his meeting with Ethan Wolf on Wednesday.

Nick was incredulous. "You really made those demands of a mobster? A guy you know is a killer?"

"I thought it'd work, Nick. We kinda had him backed into a corner. And I think it did work. Wolf called me back today to say Spinelli agreed to it." Owen explained how part of the money had been wired already, with the rest scheduled to follow the next day.

"No shit! That's unbelievable. Have you told Dante's wife?"

"I'm going to wait until it's all in the account, then call her tomorrow."

"Awesome! Hey, what about your admission at Dante's funeral that you were the one who killed that guy? Can you get into any trouble over that?"

"Not really, Sully. First of all, I'm not sure who's even going to hear about it. I'm sure some of the people who were there will talk, but it may never get to the police or DA. And even if it did, the crime they charged Dante with was involuntary manslaughter. And unlike murder, that does have a statute of limitations, which expired seven years ago."

"What about your family? They gonna deal with this OK?"

"They'll be fine, Sully. What are they gonna do, disown me? Besides, most people have some skeleton in their closet," he said, thinking of his mother, who had stopped drinking eight years ealier. "That makes them a little more understanding dealing with other people's skeletons."

"Could this cause you any problems at work?"

"I seriously doubt it. Odds are no one here will even hear about it," said Owen. "And I don't think a one-time mistake that happened ten years ago would undo whatever goodwill I've built up here over the last few years. I'm not worried about it, Sully."

"Man, it still hasn't even sunk in that this nightmare is over. Damn! Listen, you gotta come to the game Saturday night. Then we'll go out afterward to celebrate a little." He paused briefly. "And raise a toast to Dante."

"That sounds good, Sully. I'll call you tomorrow after the rest of the money comes in. And we can work out the details for Saturday night."

* * *

Friday was the first routine day Owen or Nick had enjoyed in a couple of weeks. Owen resumed his habit of walking to work, and Nick was able to concentrate on hockey again. The $500,000 wire transfer hit the trust account around noon on Friday. Owen left a message for Wolf and also talked to Nick to let him know things were wrapped up and to make plans for Saturday night. After going out for dinner and a few beers with some friends from work, Owen lay in bed on Friday night thinking about how wonderful it felt simply to have his normal life back.

Chapter 39

Sitting in the locker room at Boston's TD Garden at 6:55 on Saturday evening, ten minutes before game time, Nick was massaging his bothersome right calf. Taping his stick in the locker next to him, Henrik Lindberg noticed this.

"Are you going to be alright tonight, Sully?"

"Yeah, Lindy, I'll be fine. Just gotta get it stretched out a bit."

Privately, though, Nick was a bit concerned. The calf had bothered him all week. And though he thought he could get it stretched out during the pregame warm-ups, it remained tight and sore. There was no question he'd play, but he wondered how effective he'd be.

Back at his locker two and a half hours later, Nick felt silly for worrying about his leg before the game. Once the puck dropped, the added intensity and adrenaline helped loosen his calf, and by his third shift he felt 100 percent healthy. He wound up playing one of his best games of the season, scoring one goal, assisting on another, and leading his team in both blocked shots and hits. A big night from the Bruins' top line combined with a rare off game by the Red Wings goalie, however, combined to produce a 4–3 overtime win for the Bruins.

Spinelli watched the game from one of his regular hangouts, the Horseshoe Pub in Revere. He watched the game only because he was a big Bruins fan, not because he had any financial interest in it. Once he learned that

Nick would not throw the game, he had managed to cancel most of his bets; and for those bets he couldn't back out of, he effectively canceled them by placing the same size bets on the Red Wings with a different bookie. He had also warned Jensen to do the same. That had not been a pleasant conversation.

Sitting at the bar with Carmine Benevento, Spinelli grew increasingly angry as the game wore on. His ire resulted predominantly from his bitterness over having his scheme thwarted. Six beers and three shots of Jack Daniels added fuel to the fire. When the Bruins scored in overtime to win the game, the bar at the Horseshoe Pub erupted in cheers. That pushed the enraged Spinelli over the edge, as he thought of all the money he would've won if he'd kept his bets in place. He picked up a shot glass and hurled it at the mirror behind the bar, shattering it. He then stormed out of the bar. Benevento gave $500 to the bartender—who knew who Spinelli was and knew better than to make an issue out of the mirror—and followed Spinelli outside.

Benevento found Spinelli leaning against Benevento's car, muttering to himself. His mood did not appear to have improved. Benevento used his remote to unlock the doors, and they both got in.

"Where to, Vinnie?"

"Just take me fuckin' home, man. I'm in no mood to go any other fuckin' place."

"You got it, Vinnie."

After getting dropped off at his townhouse, Spinelli went inside and poured himself three fingers of Jim Beam. He then grabbed one of his disposable cell phones and dialed a number.

* * *

Owen was waiting for Nick when he emerged from the TD Garden locker room. After exchanging heartfelt hugs, they headed to a late dinner at Del Frisco's, an upscale steakhouse in Boston's burgeoning seaport district. Nick was often quiet, even distracted, after games, as he tended to replay the contests in his head. But tonight there was a lot to talk about, and he and Owen engaged in a spirited, sometimes emotional conversation throughout dinner, which they continued for another hour at the bar after their meal. It was one o'clock in the morning before Nick returned to his hotel.

Nick made it a habit of turning his phone off when he went out after a game, preferring to avoid interruptions. When he got back to his hotel room, he checked his phone and noticed three missed calls—one from his father; one from Del Blanco, the trainer; and one from a number he didn't recognize. Exhausted both physically and mentally, he decided to wait until the morning to check his voice mail.

* * *

The Red Wings' team bus was leaving the hotel at nine o'clock on Sunday morning, headed to Hanscom Airfield to catch the charter flight back to Detroit. Nick slept until almost eight thirty and then scrambled to pack his things and get down to the lobby on time. It was on the bus ride to the airport that he got around to listening to his voice mails. The first two were brief and routine— his father calling to offer his congratulations on the game Nick had played and Del Blanco checking in on his calf. When Nick heard the voice on the third voice mail, he felt chills run down his spine.

"Hey, motherfucker, I know you know who this is. I thought we had a deal, and then you fuckin' backed out on me. I don't like people who don't keep their word to me. I woulda won a shitload of money and got something else I want real bad if you had gone along with my plan. But you and your smartass friend had to fuck things up for me. And then, to make it even worse, your worthless sack of shit team had to lose anyway! That just fuckin' rubs my face in it, thinkin' about what I woulda had if I kept those bets in place. I'm pissed, man, I'm fuckin' pissed. And you and your cocksucker friend aren't goin' to get away with this shit. You're a *dead man*, Sullivan, and so is your fuckin' friend!"

Sitting on the team bus, Nick was in no position to talk to Owen about the voice mail. So he sent him a text: "Spinelli left me a voice mail last night. Sounded pissed. Says he's going to kill us both. Can't talk now, call you when I get to Detroit. Till then, watch your back."

Owen was eating a light breakfast at home when he received Nick's text. He sent him a quick reply, asking him to call as soon as he could. Deciding to eschew his usual Sunday-morning run, Owen hunkered down to wait for Nick's call and think things through.

* * *

The Red Wings' flight touched down at Detroit Metro Airport a few minutes after noon. Nick was in his car by twelve thirty and immediately called Owen.

"Hey, Sully, you alone?" asked Owen when he picked up.

"Yeah, I'm in my car."

"I can't believe this. You're sure it was him?"

"Definitely. That's not a voice I'm going to forget real soon."

"He sounded serious? I mean, you really think he meant he was going to actually kill us?"

"Jeez, Owen, I can't read his mind. All I can tell you is, one, he sounded really pissed. And two, he said we're both dead. I think his actual words were something like, 'You're a dead man, Sullivan, and so is your smartass friend.'"

"Shit," said Owen. "I thought this thing was over."

"Owen, I think you should do what you threatened to do. Tell your lawyer he can tell what's-his-name, Spinelli's boss, about what Spinelli was planning."

"If we do that, Sully, there's a good chance we're basically setting up Spinelli for murder."

"And the problem with that is…? Owen, this guy tried to make me sell out my teammates and throw a goddamn NHL game. Then, he *murdered* Dante. And on top of that, he welches on your deal with him and threatens to kill both of us. If this guy got killed, I wouldn't lose one second of sleep over it. The world'd be a better place."

Owen was silent for a moment. "It's hard to argue with that, Nick. I guess my only hesitation is, what if he was just drunk and pissed off, and threatened to kill us in the heat of the moment, but he was just blowing off steam—he isn't really going to come after us."

"You want to take that chance, Owen?" asked Nick. "This is not a guy who deserves the benefit of the doubt."

"You may be right. Let me just think about it a little more, OK?"

"Just do your thinking fast, OK? You never know how quick this guy will act."

"I'll call you later today. Are you gonna be around?"

"Yeah. I got practice from four o'clock till about five thirty, but I'll be around before and after that. Call me whenever you're ready."

* * *

After hanging up with Nick, Owen absently walked from his kitchen into his living room, lost in thought. On a whim, he pulled back the curtain to his front window and looked down onto Grove Street. Parking was permitted on the side of Grove Street on which Owen's condo was located, but the other side of the street was a no-parking zone. Owen noticed a car illegally parked on the opposite side of the street, about twenty yards to the right of his front entrance. It was a black Ford Explorer.

Deciding that the best thing to do was clear his head for a little while, Owen grabbed his laptop and read through a couple of memos and a due-diligence report on a project he was supervising at work. An hour later, he stood up to stretch and again peeked out the window. The Explorer was still there. Its windows were tinted, preventing him from seeing inside it.

After thinking things through for a few minutes, Owen decided to press matters a bit. There was moderate foot traffic on Grove Street, befitting a Sunday afternoon, so Owen was confident that if the Explorer did contain Spinelli's men, they would not kill him or grab him in broad daylight on Grove Street. Instead, he figured, they were probably watching to see if he entered his condo, so they could move against him there, or waiting to follow him to a more vulnerable location. So Owen headed downstairs, took a left outside his front door, and walked briskly up Grove Street, away from where the Explorer was parked.

At the first intersection, he took a right onto Revere Street, crossing Grove Street, which afforded him an opportunity to look discreetly back toward his condo. The

Explorer was inching forward in his direction. Revere Street was a one-way street, with traffic flowing opposite to the direction Owen was walking in, so the Explorer could not follow him down that street; it continued straight up Grove Street instead. Owen quickly circled the block, peeking around the corner at each intersection to make sure there was no sign of the Explorer, and was back inside his building less than five minutes after he left it.

The first thing Owen did after entering his condo was pull the curtains back half an inch from the corner of his living room window and check the street, just in time to see the Explorer edging back into its previous spot. The second thing he did was call Nick.

"Hey, Owen, what's up?"

"I'm going to do it, Sully. I'm going to tell Brogna I'm waiving the attorney-client privilege."

"Glad to hear it, Owen. We gotta be thinking about each other and ourselves here, not about Spinelli."

"You're right. By the way, be careful out there. I'm pretty sure Spinelli's guys are sitting outside my condo."

"Shit, Owen, what're you gonna do?" exclaimed Nick.

"It'll be fine, Sully. I'm not leaving the building as long as the car's still there. And I'm sure as hell not opening my door for anyone. The car's illegally parked, so it won't be able to stay there too long—the meter maids around here are vicious. Those guys are just looking for an opportunity to get at me without anyone around. I'll make sure I don't give them one."

"OK. I'll check in with you when I get outa practice later today."

Making sure to keep his distance from any windows, Owen grabbed his laptop, composed a brief e-mail to Joe Brogna, and then hit "send."

* * *

Brogna was at home in the well-heeled town of Wellesley, reading a Jonathan Franzen novel in his opulent den, when his cell phone buzzed to signal an incoming e-mail. A glance at his phone told him the e-mail was from Owen, and he put down his book and opened the e-mail.

> Mr. Brogna: With this e-mail, I am waiving all attorney-client privileges with respect to any information I provided to you during our meeting in your Boston office last Tuesday, February 4. As we discussed during that meeting, I understand that this means you are free to disclose that information to whomever you wish.
>
> Thank you for your assistance on the matter for which I engaged you. It is proving to be invaluable.

Owen Anderson

Brogna then scrolled through his contacts until he found the name he was looking for and hit the "dial" icon.

"Romero, it's Joe. We need to meet somewhere we can talk. Right away."

* * *

Vincent Spinelli spent much of Sunday evening at a sparsely furnished apartment in Lynn, just north of the Revere line. The occupants of the apartment were two prostitutes working for Spinelli's crew. Both of the girls were normally "on duty" that night, but Spinelli had given one of them, Miranda, the night off. It wasn't really a night off; she was simply plying her trade on a single client rather than a series of them—and a nonpaying one at that. In the best tradition of morally corrupt bosses, Spinelli was not shy about diverting his organization's resources for his personal use.

Driving home from Miranda's apartment, Spinelli's thoughts were occupied by Nick and Owen. The failure of his game-fixing scheme and the brazen manner in which Owen had backed him down had really struck a nerve. He was determined to kill both of them. Exacting revenge on them would scratch a severe itch for him. But beyond that, in his line of work, it was critical to strike back hard at people who fucked with you; otherwise, the whole world would be in line to fuck with you. At least that's what he told himself.

It was just after eleven o'clock on Sunday night when Spinelli eased his Porsche into the garage under his Revere townhouse. Preoccupied with thinking about how to get to Sullivan when no one was around, he didn't hear the first few footsteps emerging from the darkness at the back of his garage. He was almost to the door leading into his townhouse when he first heard a sound behind him. It was the last sound he'd ever hear.

Made in the USA
Coppell, TX
20 September 2022